THE BREAKFAST BURGER MURDER

A Burger Bar Mystery Book 4

ROSIE A. POINT

The Breakfast Burger Murder
A Burger Bar Mystery Book 4

Copyright © 2019 by Rosie A. Point.

www.rosiepointbooks.com

All Rights Reserved. This publication or parts thereof may not be reproduced in any form, stored, distributed, or transmitted in any form—electronic, mechanical, photocopy, recording or otherwise—except in the case of brief quotations for review purposes.

This is a work of fiction. Any resemblance to actual persons alive or deceased, places, or events is coincidental.

Cover by Mariah Sinclair | TheCoverVault.com

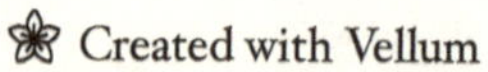
Created with Vellum

YOU'RE INVITED!

Hi there, reader!

I'd like to formally invite you to join my awesome community of readers. We love to chat about cozy mysteries, cooking, and pets.

It's super fun because I get to share chapters from yet-to-be-released books, fun recipes, pictures, and do give-aways with the people who enjoy my stories the most.

So whether you're a new reader or you've been enjoying my stories for a while, you can catch up with other like-minded readers, and get lots of cool content by visiting my website at *www.rosiepointbooks.com* and signing up for my mailing list.

Or simply search for me on *www.bookbub.com* and follow me there.

I look forward to getting to know you better.

Let's get into the story!

Yours,
Rosie

I had never been big on celebrating birthdays, but I could get used to this.

Breakfast in bed with an Agatha Christie novel, and the pet kitty of the house, Curly Fries, locked out of my room while I enjoyed this moment on my own. It was the most peaceful I'd been in Sleepy Creek, and it was definitely the best birthday I'd had.

I hummed and cut into the Breakfast Burger Grizzy had served me this morning. The runny yolk oozed and mingled beautifully with the juicy hamburger patty. The tomatoes were a ripe red, fresh and ever so slightly sweet. The bun had been toasted to perfection and was dotted with sesame seeds.

Overall, it was about the best meal I could have asked for.

I took a bite off the end of my fork and chewed

enthusiastically, smiling to myself as I turned another page in the paperback.

The vicar had found the dead body of the most hated guy in the town. A classic, the first in the Miss Marple series, and my favorite book by far.

A knock rattled at my bedroom door, and Grizzy opened it and slipped inside. "Happy birthday!" she said, for the fifth time this morning. "Have I mentioned how happy I am you're still here?"

"Thank you," I said, and put my book down, carefully marking my place with a marker. "Griz, you didn't have to go through all this trouble for me. I—"

Grizzy whipped out a package from behind her back and held it out. It was small, wrapped in golden paper and with a big cream bow on top.

"Wow, Griz, you really didn't have to." I couldn't remember the last time someone had gotten me a gift. My throat grew tight. "Really. This is too much. Breakfast and a gift?"

"Come on, just open it." She walked it over to me, and Curly Fries slipped through the crack in the open door behind her. Of course, the cat would take her opportunity to taunt me on my birthday. It wasn't enough that I was officially one year past thirty.

"Thank you." I took the present and tore the gift wrap off. I lifted a book, admiring its glossy cover. "Murder on the Orient Express."

"I figured it was time you retired that worn out copy of Miss Marple and move onto Poirot."

"Griz, this is awesome."

She came over and gave me a hug. I squeezed her back.

"I'm spoiled today. I've never been treated like this before."

"Chris, that makes me kind of sad. Everyone should be treated well on their birthday. Even if—no! No, no, no, Curly, you know you're not allowed in here. No burgers for you."

"It's fine," I said.

Grizzy looked at me like I'd grown an extra head. "What do you mean it's fine? You hate it when she stares at you."

"She can stay for now."

"Oh. Oh, all right, your funeral," Griz said, and laughed at my expression. "I didn't mean it like that."

It wasn't easy to take jokes about death or funerals too lightly nowadays. Sleepy Creek had seen its fair share of murders over the course of the last month. Just last week, I'd fallen into another investigation, one that might have involved the same people who had murdered my mother years ago.

"Christie?"

"Huh? Sorry." I often thought of my mom at times like these. My birthday, especially. I wished she was here to celebrate with me. *She'd have loved this burger.*

"I've got to get to the Burger Bar," Griz said. "But you enjoy your day off. Don't let Curly irritate you too much."

"Nothing can bother me today," I said.

Griz hopped up, dusted off her blue jeans, checked that her uniform shirt with its Burger Bar logo on the breast pocket was straight, then hurried from the room.

Curly took her opportunity. She leaped onto the bed and sat her fluffy butt down. She didn't flick her tail or meow, but stared at me, those yellow eyes all-seeing.

"Has anybody ever told you, you've got a face only a mother could love?" I asked, as I cut another piece of my burger. I shed the meat of its bun and egg, then speared the bit of grilled patty on the end of my fork. "But, since it's my birthday, why not?" I held out the fork to her.

Curly erupted into her food purrs and came over. She rubbed the side of her face against my hand then licked the burger. She took it off the fork with her teeth, dropped it onto my frilly pink duvet cover, and set to work feasting.

I would've been irritated if I hadn't thought the meat stain improved the duvet set. "There," I said. "Now, you get a birthday gift from me on my birthday." I flipped the paperback over in my hand and read the blurb as I spoke. "And your birthday gift to me can be not sleeping on my head tonight. Or leaving anymore mice in my shoes. Deal?"

She didn't look up from her feast.

A bang rang out downstairs.

"What the…?" I shifted my breakfast tray aside.

Thudding steps ascended the stairs, and my heart did a flip, turn and a double-dip. *Spiders?* I hopped out of bed and positioned myself behind the door.

It flew open and banged into my nose.

"Christie!" Grizzy called.

"Ow." I lifted my hand and covered my face. "Ow, ow, ow, what was that for?"

"Hey, wait, why are you behind the door?"

"Because I thought you were—"

My friend grabbed my wrist and pulled me back to the bed, then forced me onto it. "It doesn't matter," she said. "You need to get dressed, now."

"What?"

Grizzy stormed to my dresser drawers and ripped them open. She grabbed an armful of clothing, marched back over to me and threw it in my lap. "Quickly. We've got to go."

"What? Where?"

Even Curly was shocked. She'd stopped eating long enough to meow balefully at Griselda.

"The hospital."

"Why?"

"Because I got a call from Vee as I was on my way out the door. Nelly Boggs has been attacked. And her mother has been … well, it's not looking good."

"What?" I leaped up from the bed and showered the floor in clothing and underwear. "Please tell me you're kidding." Nelly was a sweetheart who'd done nothing but spread good will since I'd first met her. The florist. Who would attack her and why?

"I'm not kidding," she said. "Come on. We've got to meet Missi and Vee there in five minutes." And then Grizzy was out of my room again, the door slamming shut behind her.

An attack on Nelly? And her mother was, what, dead? *Not again.*

I dressed fast then rushed out of the room and down to Grizzy's waiting Kia, my heart thumping in my chest.

❧ 2 ❧

"What is it about hospital cafeterias?" Missi asked, and took a tight-lipped sip from her Styrofoam cup. "You'd think they'd have the best coffee, what with all those handsome exhausted doctors running around, but no. No, it's just... swill."

"I happen to agree, for once." Virginia placed her half-empty cup on our melamine-topped table. "How much longer do you think we'll have to wait?"

We had gathered in the cafeteria to wait for visiting hours. Nelly was alive and recovering from a bump on the head, but the same couldn't be said for her mother. The cops had already come to the hospital to take Nelly's testimony because Martha Boggs was dead.

"—as soon as they're finished," Grizzy said. "I'm just

so sad this has happened. And on Christie's birthday too."

"My birthday's got nothing to do with it," I said. "What matters now is we rally around poor Nelly. She's been through so much already, what with losing Francesca and now this." It was a little too close to home for me. I'd lost my mother in Sleepy Creek years ago.

"Yes, it's terrible," Vee said. "I hope the police finish soon, so we can get in there and— Oh! Look, there's that detective of yours, Christie."

I stiffened.

Liam Balle, the detective who'd just so happened to have asked me out on a date last weekend at the Food Fair, stood in the doorway, his gaze traveling over the diners and doctors and nurses.

He spotted me then sauntered over and stopped next to our table. "Morning, ladies."

"Good morning, detective Balle," Griz, Vee and Missi chorused.

I cringed inwardly. "Hi. What's up?"

"Talk to you for a second?" Balle asked.

"In an official or unofficial capacity?" I rose, not really expecting an answer, and followed him across the cafeteria to an empty table. He drew out a chair for me then took one himself.

"Thanks." I tried not to blush like a bruised tomato. "So, what's going on?"

"See, now, that's exactly what I wanted to talk to *you* about." Balle ran a thumb over his chin, dragging it along stubble. Too tired to shave? Perhaps, he'd been called out of bed early? "It's a murder. Martha Boggs was shot, and I'm only telling you that, Christie, because it's already been printed in the papers and released online."

"You want me to butt out," I said.

"I want you to not wind up in trouble. You've escaped danger and being fired from your job by the skin of your teeth three times now. No one's that lucky."

"I'm like a cat," I said, grinning at him. "I've got nine lives."

His dark eyes narrowed. "And what does curiosity do to cats?"

"There was another part of that idiom. I believe it involved satisfaction."

"Don't be cute with me," he said, but his tone wasn't nearly as gruff as it had been when we'd first met. "You know I've got to do the right thing."

"And so do I. And if doing the right thing involves staying clear of trouble, including whatever's going on with Nelly and Martha, or was going on with Martha before she died, then there's nothing for you to worry about."

"Evasive."

"What did you expect?" I asked. "Nelly's my friend."

The corners of Liam's lips twitched upward, and his handsome quotient grew by one hundred points.

"What?" I asked.

"Nothing, just, it's funny."

"What is?"

"When you came to Sleepy Creek you were just the detective and the out-of-towner. Now, you're a part of this place," Liam said.

"Let's not get ahead of ourselves here." But that brought another question to light—if I wasn't a part of the town, then why was I here, flirting with the detective? If I couldn't stay, what was the point of going on a date with him?

Relax. It's no big deal.

Liam sighed. "Well, I tried. And I don't need to warn you that—"

"If you catch me investigating, you'll have to report me and arrest me for real this time," I said.

"Correct."

But there was a big 'if' in that sentence. If he caught me. He wouldn't. I had to be truthful with myself—I wanted to find out what had happened to my mother and now, to Nelly and her mother. The more I tried to deny it, the more impulsive I became in my investigations.

This time around I'd be clear-headed, and maybe, I'd help solve this case without getting caught.

"Oh boy," Balle said. "I can see the dials whirring in that pretty head of yours."

"Pretty?"

"What, you never looked in a mirror before?" He winked at me as he rose from the table. "Stay out of trouble, Chris."

And then he was gone, and I was left with a fluttering heart. So not me. I gave myself a second to calm down before heading back over to the table. The women looked at me, interest sparkling in their eyes. Missi's mouth was halfway open, likely with a barbed comment on the tip of her tongue.

"Before anyone says anything"—I lifted my palm—"I think we can go see Nelly now. Visiting hours. Cops are gone. Let's go."

"Don't think you're getting out of this that easily," Missi said.

"It's my birthday. You're not allowed to tease me on my birthday."

"I did not sign anything with that stated on it." But Missi didn't start up the Liam-related line of questioning.

We made our way through the Logan's Rest Hospital, down sterile corridors, while nurses or doctors or patients passed by. We took the elevator to the second floor and found Nelly in her ward. She was sharing with three others and two empty beds.

Nelly's mousy brown hair fell around her face, as

usual, but a huge bandage had been tied around the top of it that made her look a lot like a cheesy mummy from an old silent film. She was propped up against her pillows, TV remote in hand, and a smile on her face.

"There you are," she said. "The detectives mentioned that you four tried to barge in here before they could."

"Visiting hours have started, at last," Grizzy replied. "How are you feeling, Nelly?"

"I'm fine. A little bit headachey, but the doctor says that if I take my meds and get lots of rest, I'll be out of here in no time. By tonight. I'm looking forward to that. I've never liked hospitals. Could you close the curtains?" She gestured to the sheets surrounding her bed.

Missi swept the baby blue curtains closed and shuddered. I didn't blame her. The last time we'd been here Virginia had been the one in the hospital bed.

We huddled around her, and I struggled to keep my face straight. Why was Nelly so happy? Surely, the detectives had told her what had happened to her mother. How could I ask Nelly about her mom without coming off too much like a detective?

I nudged Grizzy. She was the one who was good with emotions.

"How are you feeling... emotionally?" Grizzy asked, and took a chair at the head of Nelly's bed, right next to her little counter-cupboard combo. A vase of flowers sat there with a card perched among the roses. Fitting, since Nelly was a florist.

Nelly chewed on her bottom lip. "You're worried because of my mother?"

Aren't you?

"I mean," Nelly said, "I'm sad that she's dead, but I just, well, this isn't going to sound great, but my mother and I weren't that close. Not as close as we could have been. So I'm sad, but I'm not beat up about it. I guess the worst thing about it is, I was just getting to know her again. We never really had a relationship, and this was our chance. She'd finally bought a house in Sleepy Creek and wanted to get to know me."

"Sorry Nelly," Missi said.

I echoed the sentiment.

"Yes, our sincerest condolences." Virginia patted Nelly on the arm. "Grief comes in all shapes and sizes. You might not feel poorly now, and that's good, but if you ever do need support, you know where to find us."

Nelly's eyes swam with tears, and she looked down at her hands, fiddling with the remote control. She lifted it and muted the TV overhead. "T-thank you. I think I've taken some strength from all of you. So much has happened in Sleepy Creek recently, and you all have been pillars of strength. Look at Christie, her life is falling apart, and she's so strong."

"Gee, thanks," I said.

Missi snorted. "Shoe fits, wear it."

The other women took seats too, but I remained standing at the end of Nelly's bed. "What happened, Nelly?" I asked. "If you don't mind me asking. I know you've probably had to go over it with the detectives."

"I don't mind. I trust the detectives, but you've gotten great results for me in the past. I mean, you solved Fran's murder when I asked for your help. And I have the horrible suspicion that the police will want to blame me for this again."

Odd. Why would she worry about that? She should have been more concerned about the fact that her family member had died.

Easy. One step at a time.

"My mom recently bought an estate in the wealthier suburbs."

"Oh, you mean in 'Money Bags Town?'" That was what the citizens of Sleepy Creek called it. The area where all the richie riches lived and kept their wealth. I'd visited the long winding road that led between estates on a previous case. Even the air smelled green.

"Yes, well, my mother was wealthy, and she bought an estate from Mr. Huxley last month. She moved in about a week ago. I was meant to have dinner with her, but when I arrived at the house, the front door was open and it was dark inside. I called out for my mom, but there was no answer."

I held the railing at the end of the bed. "What happened then?"

"A man, or a woman, I don't know which because they had a mask on, came rushing out of the hall. They were skinny, and they had a gun in their hand, and they bashed past me and threw me down. That's the last thing I remember. Next thing I knew, I was waking up here."

"That's just terrible, Nelly." Grizzy stroked our friends' arm.

"That's really all I know. If I remember anything else, I'll tell you." Nelly lay back, and the others started up talking to her about happier things.

I didn't join in, but offered a smile every now and again.

A masked attacker in Sleepy Creek? It was too much, too soon. There had been four murders since I'd arrived, and some of them were definitely connected to my mother's death twelve years ago.

Was it the same for this case?

There was only one way to find out.

※ 3 ※

"We've got another order for the Breakfast Burger," I cried, and rang the bell in the kitchen window. "Sunny side up, make that egg yolk lovely and runny, Jarvis."

"Comin' right up, mon."

Jarvis was always cool as a cucumber, even though he had a mountain of orders waiting. The man was a wonder in the kitchen, a Jamaican chef genius who came up with new burgers every week. And he was a part of the reason my waistline had expanded these past three weeks.

To be fair, that was partly Griselda's fault. She made a mean pie, and soup, and filet mignon. Gosh, my friend could have been a chef in her own right. It was no wonder her cat was overweight. I'd started sympathizing with Curly Fries. A stance I'd never thought I'd take.

But, like Curly, I'd have to go on a diet. Simple as that.

I swept back to my table and grinned at the new waiter, Hedy, on the way past. She'd started last week and had finally gotten the hang of things. Soft-spoken and sweet, she probably got better tips than I did.

"Can I get you anything else, Mr. Krebbler?" I asked, stopping next to the crotchety old man's table.

He wasn't my least favorite customer, but he was on the list. Then again, I couldn't blame him for being a grump. I was one myself.

"You didn't put the cherry on my milkshake," he said. "Why not?"

"Mr. Krebbler, there was definitely a cherry on your malt shake," I said, nodding toward the bar at the back of the restaurant. The retro vibe was strong in this place, and every puffy, vinyl stool was occupied by a customer. "See? Griselda's making shakes right now."

And, indeed, my bestie had two shakes on the counter and was in the process of depositing a cherry on the mound of cream on top of each one.

"I asked for two cherries," Krebbler said, pursing his wrinkly lips. "Two cherries. Service in here is going downhill. Sleepy Creek too. Another woman murdered, and it's barely been a week since the last incident. Shouldn't even be out and about with times like these.

Might get murdered in here. Might get murdered while I'm walking down the street."

"Or hit by lightning." I gestured to the sunny, blue skies outside. "Come on, Mr. Kreb, things will be fine. This is just another hiccup in Sleepy Creek's road to recovery."

"Kreb? Did you just call me Kreb?"

I sighed. "I can get you another cherry, you know. I'm sure Grizzy won't charge you extra for it."

"That's not the point." Krebbler narrowed already beady eyes at me. "You know, I've got my suspicions about you."

"I'd love to hear them. I'm fueled by suspicions."

"You've got a bad attitude," he said. "No tip for you."

"I'm shattered, Mr. Krebbler. I'll be right back with your single cherry." I fumed my way over to the bar, forcing a smile that scared more than it welcomed. A few of the other customers recoiled at the look on my face.

"Uh oh," Grizzy said, as she placed two milkshakes on Hedy's serving tray. "The Kreb giving you trouble?"

"Is the sky blue?"

"What does he want this time?"

"To drive me to madness. Or to see me bald from pulling my hair out. And a cherry. A single cherry on a plate, please. Better yet, put it on a silver platter if you have one."

Grizzy laughed as she removed a cherry, put it on a plate, and handed it over to me. I thanked her then swept back to the Kreb's table. "Here you are, Mr. Krebbler. Here's your cherry. Lovely and sweet to make your day better."

"I meant what I said." Krebbler lifted the plate and eyed his cherry. "About my suspicions. About you."

"Oh?" I glanced at the other tables in the Burger Bar. Some of them needed my help and the longer I spent chatting to the cherry-aficionado, the worse things got for them. And for me.

"Things only started going downhill after you arrived in town. Don't think I didn't notice that. I've got my eye on you, miss."

"I'll sleep easier knowing that. Do you need anything else, Mr. Krebbler?"

He drew in air through his hooked nose. "Not yet."

"Enjoy your cherry, sir."

I spent the rest of the morning rush tending to my tables and trying to keep my cool whenever Krebbler asked me for something else. I had to put up a brave face, or a smiling one, and did it for Grizzy. This was her restaurant, and I didn't want to be the reason customers didn't come back.

Breakfast Burgers were the talk of the restaurant, with people ordering them one after the other. It was a miracle Jarvis was still on his feet by the time the restaurant cleared out a little and breakfast turned to the quiet period before brunch.

I sat down on one of the barstools to rest my feet, and Grizzy whipped me up a break-time milkshake. "Tough morning," she said. "I've never made so many shakes."

"Spring has sprung, and summer is on its way, and weirdly, the murders don't seem to be deterring the tourists."

"That's because they're intrigued," Grizzy said. "Or the papers aren't doing it justice. And it's the Sleepy Creek way. You know, keep going. Carry on. Everything will be fine as long as we have our burgers and our milkshakes."

"A good burger solves any problem," Jarvis called from the kitchen.

"Hear, hear." Grizzy slid my milkshake over

I plopped a thick paper straw into it and slurped some down, relishing the cool sweetness. "Have you heard from Nelly?"

"Only that she's being discharged today."

"We should go see her sometime," I said.

Grizzy gave me the look. The 'I know what you're up to, you dirty little investigator' look that she wore so well.

"What?"

"I don't even have to say not to investigate," Grizzy

sighed. "I won't waste my breath. You're not going to do what's good for you."

"Investigating *is* good for me."

The bell above the door rang, and I caught the reflection of Liam entering the restaurant. My cheeks grew pink, right away. Gosh, I had to get control of myself. There were more important things than mooning away over an incredibly handsome man.

In uniform.

Ahem.

I slurped on my milkshake so hard, that a clot of thick ice cream, shot free of the straw and right up against the roof of my mouth. I choked and spluttered.

"You all right there, Christie?" Liam took the seat next to mine at the bar. "Hiya, Griselda, can I get one of your special burgers to go. And a choc shake?"

"Sure, no problem." Grizzy gave the order to Jarvis while I tried to recover what remained of my dignity.

"How are you?" Liam asked me. "Apart from the brain freeze."

"I'm fine. Tired. Been busy in here. What about you? You doing good?" Gosh, why were my sentences so short? I had to relax.

"I'm fine. Stress at work, but that comes with the job description at the moment."

"More pressure from your captain about the murders?"

Liam raised an eyebrow at me.

"I'm asking as a friend," I said. "Not because I want to get involved."

"I'll believe that... never." He laughed. "And friend? Is that what we are? Friends?"

"I mean, I hope so. I don't consider you my enemy, but the jury's out on that one."

"I'm sure I told you not to get cute with me," he said, and offered me another smile. It was such a rare thing to see from him. At least, when it came to me. He was usually gruff and angry that I'd interfered. "I'll admit I came in here with an ulterior motive."

"You want answers? I wish I knew anything that would help you. Nelly mentioned a gun, and that she didn't see who her attacker was. And that her mother recently bought a mansion in 'Money Bags Town.' I mean, Foldmead."

Liam put a hand on my arm. "Not what I meant by ulterior motive. I asked you out on a date, last week at the Fair? So, let's organize a time. What do you say we head out tonight? I know a great little place in Logan's Rest that doesn't serve pizza or burgers."

"Hard sell," I replied, my heart thumping along. "But OK. Yeah, that sounds good. What time?"

"7pm good for you?"

"Sure."

"I'll see you then, Christie." He removed his wallet

from his pocket and paid for his order, then went to sit at one of the tables to wait for his food.

I barely kept a straight face as Griselda gave me wide eyes and jostled up and down on the spot. "You're going on a date," she whispered.

Funnily enough, I was more nervous for a date with Liam than I was for investigating the murder of Martha Boggs. Perhaps, I could use the date as an opportunity to squeeze Liam for information. If I could keep myself from blushing and staring at him like a google-eyed doll for more than two minutes.

4

The plan to go see Nelly was postponed until tomorrow, when I'd have to take Curly Fries on her weight-loss walk. Because tonight was all about my date with Liam. And it was weird. Oh boy, I hadn't put more than mascara on in ages, yet here I was, seated across from him in a fancy-schmance restaurant wearing a full face. Never mind the pretty dress Griselda had forced me into, insisting that I had to look more like a lady than a cop for this.

Apparently, jeans, sneakers and a t-shirt didn't fit the date aesthetic.

The place in Logan's Rest was nice. A Mediterranean restaurant with pasta dishes and tapas and gosh, delicious food that smelled so good my mouth watered.

"Thanks for picking this place out," I said, and smiled at Liam. "It's not what I expected."

"Well, it took us a while to get here because of the drive, but I heard this place is great for date nights." Liam wore a button-down shirt and a little too much gel in his hair. I had my suspicions that Arthur, Grizzy's boyfriend, had had some input in his outfit too.

The waiter had already placed a plate of crusty bread on the table, and Balle had shown me a trick—oil and balsamic in a saucer. Drag the bread through it and eat. It was surprisingly tasty, but nothing beat butter on bread in my humble opinion.

I scooped another slice through the concoction and delivered it to my mouth. "This is good," I said.

"Yeah, not what I expected, but great. I can't wait for our appetizers to come."

"You know, I wouldn't have pegged you as the foodie type."

"I live in Sleepy Creek," Liam replied. "Even if I wasn't when I first arrived, I sure am now. Can't stay in the foodie capital of Ohio for long without becoming a convert."

"Foodie capital is a stretch. But I get what you mean." The conversation was easy with him, and I hadn't been expecting that. I wasn't easy to get on with. "So, how are things with you at work?"

"I hope you're not taking this as an opportunity to interview me, Christie."

I managed to keep a straight face. I did like this guy,

even though I didn't want to. Emotions were complicated. "No, I'm just curious. The last time we spoke about it, you were stressed. You know, captain putting pressure on you to connect the murder cases since there have been so many in such a short span of time."

Liam gave a grunt. "It's still the same. Did you ever experience anything like this back in Boston? Shoot, is that a bad thing to ask since you're on sabbatical?"

"No, it's fine. And yeah. I did, and I did stupid stuff trying to prove myself, hence the fact that I'm here. But … pressure does strange things to people."

"Murderous things," Liam said, and glanced sideways. He froze for the briefest of moments, his eyebrows drawing inward, and his gaze fixed on the table across from ours.

"What?" I asked.

"Nothing."

A woman sat at that table—blonde hair with big hoop earrings and pale pink lipstick. She kind of reminded me of a Barbie doll with less plastic. *That's Janine Huxley.* I recognized her from the Burger Bar.

She'd come in a few weeks ago to petition us to introduce an all-vegan menu. Grizzy had mentioned creating a vegetarian burger, but there was no way we could shop a Burger Bar without meat.

Janine sat across from a tall guy, hunched over. Black hair, stringy hanging in his face. Pimples. Maybe just out of his teens, and definitely not the type I'd have envisioned ex-Prom Queen Janine with. She was like the younger, more attractive version of Mona Jonah.

Cross her and the retribution would be swift.

"Why are you staring at Janine?" I asked.

"Oh, nothing like that," Liam said. "I mean … I can't officially tell you why."

"Oh." Part of the case. That was interesting. Balle might be set on not giving up any information today, but he'd unwittingly just done so.

Janine Huxley. Was she a suspect? She didn't seem the murdering type, but then I'd seen enough in my short time as a detective to know that murder didn't have a type. It came in all shapes and sizes and profiles. DNA and criminal.

"Do you want to move?" I asked. "Closer? We could listen in on her conversation."

"Starting to see why you were suspended now." Liam laughed.

I did too. "Yeah, unorthodox, but I get results."

"Don't start."

The waiter returned with our tapas and we tucked into fresh olives and feta cheese, Patatas bravas with a spicy sauce, and calamares, which were crunchy squid. Everything was perfect, and we drank down sodas because Liam would have to drive us back, and I wasn't much of a drinker.

The conversation flowed easily, but once in a while, either of us would glance over at Janine's table. Balle for his reasons, and me because I was curious about why she would be a suspect. If she even was. Chances were, I would have heard about it through gossip central—in the Burger Bar—if Janine had been interviewed.

She was super popular.

"So, you were saying about the captain putting pressure on you?" I'd given up on hope that he'd share info with me, accidentally even, about Nelly's mother's murder. "Are you OK?"

"I'm fine. I'll be fine. But it makes solving these cases even more important. Can I ask you a question?"

"Shoot," I said, between spearing an olive and a bit of feta cheese with my fork.

"Do you really think your mother's case is involved in all of this?"

I chewed pensively. Swallowed. Took my time with the answer.

"I'm asking you unofficially, but if it's a lead I need to follow, one of these days I will have to interview you."

"I do honestly believe that," I said. "And it's part of the reason I've been causing trouble for you lately. As for this case, I can't say." Until I had more information on what had actually happened. "But things have been crazy in town lately. Small towns have their problems, but five murders in such rapid succession? Difficult not to assume they're connected."

Liam nodded. "I'll follow this up with you officially when the time is right. If the time is right."

We finished our meal in a warm silence, the trickle of guitar music from the speaker overhead accompanying the last few bites. It was lovely here and the evening was over too soon.

Balle drove me back to Sleepy Creek, tapping his fingers on the steering wheel and humming along to songs on the radio. My mind whirred in the meantime, fixating on Janine, why she'd been there, and how she was involved in the case.

I had to speak to Nelly about this. Perhaps, Janine had been an enemy of Martha's? Or Nelly's? Anything was possible.

Liam walked me up the front path and right to Griselda's door. We stood awkwardly, me clearing my throat, and him scuffling his shoes.

"Well, this was lovely," I said.

"I'd like to see you again. I'll call you."

"Thanks. I mean, yeah, sure. I mean, OK that's great." Wow, I was annoying when I was nervous. "Thanks for tonight," I managed, at last.

He leaned in, closer and closer, until the scent of his cologne washed over me.

The front door slapped open. "There you are!" Grizzy cried.

Liam and I sprang apart.

"I was starting to get worried." But Griselda's smile said she knew exactly what she'd intercepted. "Are you coming in for some coffee, detective?"

"No, thank you. I'd better get some rest. Murders to solve." Liam gave a faux salute, then awkwardly shook my hand. He hurried off down the path and toward his car. He drove off with another wave.

Grizzy giggled.

"Don't you start," I said.

"Christie and Liam sitting in a tree." She grabbed my arm and dragged me into the house. "OK. Spill. Everything."

"A woman never dates and tells," I said. "But I think I found out something interesting about Martha's murder..."

5

"Come on, Curly, a little faster than that." I held the end of Curly Fries' pink lead and tapped my heel on the sidewalk. It was hot as a griddle out here, and the cat had decided she wanted to take a rest on Mrs. Immelmann's lawn. "This is ridiculous," I said. "We've barely made it across the street. And I have witnesses to question."

Curly flicked her black tail at me.

"Is it water? Do you need water?" I reached into the carry bag I always brought with on our walks and took out her cutesy paw-print embossed bowl. I placed it on the grass then filled it with bottled water. "There. Drink and let's haul some fur."

Curly sniffed the water and turned up her nose.

"Typical." I waited another minute then emptied out

the water bowl and packed it away. "I'm not picking you up."

She meowed at me, but started the Curly Fries wobble I'd grown accustomed to over the past few weeks. Off she went down the sidewalk at a snail's pace.

"Look at me," I said, "I'm a homicide detective reduced to a ... cat walker. A fat cat walker. Not that there's anything wrong with walking cats." Who was I even talking to? If I wasn't careful, one of Mona's gossip circle members would spot me ambling along talking to myself and spread rumors about me.

I turned onto Main Street and headed for Nelly's florist shop. The sign hanging in the door read 'OPEN,' and I pushed my way inside, taking a reluctant Curly with me.

Nelly stood behind the counter, leaning on top of it with both elbows, reading the newspaper. Her glasses had slid down her nose, right to the tip and she pushed them up, absently.

"Hello," I called out.

Nelly yelped and jumped on the spot. "Oh, Christie. I didn't see you there."

"You didn't hear the bell ringing?" I gestured to the little bronze bell over the door.

"I was so lost in this newspaper article. It's about my mom," she said, and folded the paper in half. She stowed it away, lifting a slab of chocolate in its place. "Would you like a block? It's Belgian. My boyfriend got it for me."

"When did you get a boyfriend?" I asked, and nudged Curly Fries with the toe of my sneaker. She'd gotten one whiff of the chocolate and suddenly found her energy. I theorized that it was because she'd never had chocolate before. The forbidden fruit. She didn't understand that this particular 'fruit' could kill her.

Nelly broke off a piece of chocolate and put it in her mouth, a smile on her lips. "Mmm, delicious."

"Nelly?"

"Oh. Last week," she said. "I know it's sudden, but I really like him. A lot. And after everything that happened with Fran and Sal—well, he's been wonderful. He was the one who kept me together during that. I'm still struggling to get over Fran's death."

But not her mother's. Why was Nelly so upbeat? It didn't sit well with me. Now, sure, people handled grief in different ways, but this seemed odd. I'd lost my mother, and it bothered me to this day.

"I'll bring him over for you to meet some time. In fact, you should come and see me at the house."

"The house?" Nelly had lived in an apartment ever since I'd known her. Granted that had been only a month, but still.

"Yes, my mother's house." Nelly held out the chocolate.

"You're living in your mom's mansion?" I asked, and took a piece. I inserted it between my lips, bit down, and instantly regretted it. It was the worst chocolate I'd ever tasted. Bitter and crumbly and strangely spicy. I forced myself to chew and swallow. "Why are you—?" I choked on a crumb of chocolate.

"She left it to me. Well, to me and my brother." Nelly caught the shock in my expression. "I know. I had no idea that I had a brother either. He came with her to town and started work at the pizzeria. I've never even met him, and now I have to share, I mean, get to know him."

I frowned. "What's your brother's name?"

"Grayson. My mom showed me his picture. She was super excited for me to meet him, but I never got the chance after what happened." Nelly shrugged and took another piece of chocolate. "I'm trying not to let any of this bother me. My boyfriend says that everything happens for a reason, and I have to agree with him. The bad and the good stuff. It just seems like a healthier way to approach life."

Curly Fries meowed at the word 'healthy.'

"Well, I just came to check in on you. You're all right?"

"I'm fine, Chris, thanks for asking," Nelly said. "You and Grizzy and the twins are always so supportive of me. It feels like you've lived here forever."

She was right about that. When I thought about life back in Boston, it seemed a distant, hazed memory. But Boston wasn't the problem, right now. Martha's death was the issue at hand, and the fact that her daughter, my friend, wasn't grieving about it.

Or hiding her grief?

And she had a new mystery boyfriend. And a long lost brother who happened to be working at Sal's pizzeria. Sal who had fallen victim to the ministrations of a Somerville Spider.

It couldn't possibly be connected, could it? I'd wanted to help Nelly by looking into the case, but I'd fast moved on from that. Now, it was about protecting Sleepy Creek. These murders simply couldn't continue, and I hated to think they might be connected to my past.

"So," I said, and leaned on the countertop, wrinkling my nose at the odd smell drifting up from the chocolate. "Tell me about this brother of yours."

"There's not much to tell," Nelly said. "Just that he's young, just out of his teens, and that he doesn't really have any prospects." Nelly sounded slightly bitter as she said it. Possibly, as bitter as that horrible excuse for chocolate. "I mean, I'll have to meet him before I make any judgements. It doesn't seem fair to talk negatively about him when I don't know him."

A 'but' hovered in the air.

"But it seems to me," Nelly said, at last, "that he was

just living off our mother. Now that she's gone, he gets his payday."

"You suspect him?" I cut to the chase.

"I don't want to say that..." Nelly pressed her lips together. "But my boyfriend, Donovan? He thinks that it's really weird how they turned up and how next thing this has happened."

Donovan. I'd never heard of the guy. He had to be new in town. I had about a billion questions to ask and a cat on the end of a lead who kept meowing and batting my legs. Perhaps, it was potty time. "I'd better head out, Nelly."

"Sure. Thanks for stopping by. Like I said, you and Griz and the twins should come to the house. What about tomorrow night? For dinner?"

"Sounds perfect." I waved and led Curly out of the florist's. I had to get her home before she ruined our walk by dropping off a package I would have to retrieve with a baggie. And I had a plan in mind. One that didn't need a cat on board.

This brother intrigued me. Murder motivations ranged from the passionate to the financial and everywhere in between, but both Nelly and her brother had been written into their mother's will and benefited from her death. Both of them were prime suspects.

It was time to find out more about Mr. Grayson Boggs.

❧ 6 ❧

On the list of things I loved to do, hanging around outside a pizza place wasn't high up. Especially, when I wasn't waiting around for an order to be fulfilled. Truth was, Grizzy had mentioned she'd be making steak and potatoes tonight, and I was all about that.

Also, if I didn't cut back on the burgers and pizzas soon, I'd die of high cholesterol before I solved anything. Or wind up as big as a human-sized version of Curly Fries.

I took a seat on the bench outside Sal's Pizzeria, turning sideways and angling my Agatha Christie paperback so it'd look like I was reading rather than eyeing out the place. The afternoon sun had sunk in the sky, and the lights were on inside the pizzeria, behind the somewhat happy pizza embossing on the window.

People traveled in and out of the place.

It was great to see, and, shoot, it probably would have made Sal happy if he'd been around to see it.

"Rest in peace," I muttered.

Sal's restaurant was run by a friend of the family, Bella, who had bought it from the bank. She was a nice woman with great plans and the reason there was a new fluorescent sign blinking from the bricks above the entrance.

The sign had been the talk of the town after its install at the start of the week, but then Martha had been murdered and the gossip chain had latched onto that instead.

I turned a page, secretly despising that I hadn't read a word of it, and shifted my eyes sideways.

Another customer exited the pizzeria carrying a pie in a cardboard box. Inside, two people worked behind the counter, a young woman who wore a Sal's Pizzeria cap, and a man with dark hair that hung limply against his forehead.

I kept my expression focused, as if I couldn't get enough of the book in my hand, but my pulse ticked up a notch.

That was the same guy I'd seen at the restaurant in Logan's Rest on my date with Liam. The one who'd been seated across from Janine Huxley.

It was too much of a coincidence. It had to be the

brother.

What did that mean?

That Liam hadn't been looking at Janine at all but at the brother? That would make more sense, given that the brother had a solid motive for getting rid of Martha.

The guy was young, and he kept sweeping greasy hair back from his forehead then glancing around the store, his eyes rimmed in black eyeliner. I hadn't paid much attention to him the other night, but I took him in now.

Pale. Wearing cut-off leather gloves. He looked out of place in the Sal's Pizzeria shirt and had clearly opted out of wearing the cap with it. The girl working behind the counter said something to him, and he shrugged.

Another customer approached the pizzeria and entered, swaying up toward the front counter. Long blonde hair, a tight pair of skinny jeans and an even tighter red strappy top. She tossed her hair back, turning her head, and I caught sight of the side of her face. It was Janine, the woman who'd been seated across from Grayson at the restaurant last night.

Were they in a relationship?

My curiosity grew, but I stayed in place, watching as they talked to each other.

Grayson didn't seem particularly happy to see her. He gestured to the door, and she flicked her hair again then turned from the counter and stormed out into the street.

"—think he is?" she muttered, as she emerged.

Janine came over and sat down on the bench.

It must be my lucky day.

I shut my book on my finger. "Taking the bus?" I asked.

"This isn't a bus stop," Janine replied, and cast a disdainful look in my direction. "And do I know you?"

"Christie," I said, and extended a hand.

Her disdain transferred to my hand. "I'm Janine."

"I think we've met actually. You've been into the Burger Bar, right?"

"Oh. I know you," she said, and folded her arms. "You're the waitress that works there? My aunt Mona told me all about you."

I nearly choked on my own saliva. "Mona's your aunt?"

"On my mom's side."

"That's nice." There was no way I could come up with a better qualifier than 'nice.' It might have been weak, but that was because Mona was the queen of gossip and mean in Sleepy Creek.

"Yeah, it's whatever."

"So, have you lived here long? You stay with her?" I needed to find a segue into talking about Martha.

"Uh, yeah. I went away to college, but I'm back now. And it's temporary. She's super poor, like. Ew."

"Right." When had I lost the ability to hold a conversation with teenagers? Or twenty-year-olds?

"I live with my dad. But yeah, it's boring ever since we moved."

"It must be weird for you staying here."

"Why?" Janine raised a penciled in eyebrow. She was doused in perfume, and I forced myself to keep from pulling a face. I had a pretty sensitive nose.

"Because of what happened recently in the area. Martha died? Martha Boggs?" This had to be the most awkward conversation anyone had ever had in the history of all conversations. But, oh well. Pretending not to interrogate someone while interrogating them definitely wasn't a strength of mine.

"Oh, that? Who cares? Like, it will never happen to me."

"Why do you say that?"

"Because I don't make enemies, and I'm not a horrible woman?"

"Martha was horrible?" I asked. "I didn't know her at all. Thought she was new to town."

"Oh, she was, but, like, I knew people who knew her, and they all thought she was a really mean, terrible person. I'm not at all surprised that someone decided to murder her." Janine shifted on the bench and looked back at the pizzeria.

That's interesting. "That's sad," I said. "But it's alarming that there might be a murderer on the loose."

"Yeah, but, like, not one that wants to hurt me."

"Why do you say that?"

"Because who would want to hurt me?" Janine asked. "I'm like ... seriously, look at me. I'm who everyone wants to be. Women want to be me, and men fall in love with me. Simple as that."

"Sure, but you get weirdos out there, you know."

"Like weirdos who read books on benches on the street? Seriously? Don't you have a home to go to?"

What a charmer. "It was nice meeting you," I said. "Again."

"Whatever." Janine got up from the bench, touching a finger to her hoop earring. "Bye."

"Bye," I said, and lifted my palm to wave, belatedly.

Janine flounced back toward the pizzeria, trailing a cloud of perfume and entered. She came out a short while later with a pizza and headed off down the road.

I stayed, opening my book to fake read again. It wouldn't look right if I'd spoken to Janine and then walked off after. Finally, I closed my book, got up and dusted myself off, stretched out and faked a yawn.

I headed off down the street, back toward the suburbs, past glass-front stores displaying books or clothing or jewelry. None of it made an impression on me.

Janine was friends with Grayson, the son of Martha. Martha who had been mean, apparently, and deserved to be murdered. It was too suspicious. But I didn't have any evidence whatsoever.

This was a hunch, nothing more, nothing less. All I could do was follow through and figure out what was going on between Janine and this Grayson dude. And if it had anything to do with Martha's murder.

It was time to put my investigating cap on again. Had I ever taken it off?

7

"This is exciting," Grizzy said, as she steered her Kia up to the front of the mansion's gates. Thankfully, they weren't pearly as well, or I'd have been in for a swift rejection given my recent activities.

Vee and Missi were in the back, occasionally whispering about something or the other—a bit of gossip to share about a mansion we'd passed or the owner of it.

Nelly's grand manor sat further back, glimpsed between trees in bloom. The lights were on its many windows, and the door thrown open, allowing light to creep out into the purple dusk that had settled over Sleepy Creek and its infamous 'Money Bags Town.'

The forensic department over in Logan's Rest—Sleepy Creek didn't have one of its own—had already been through the crime scene and removed the tape. But the mansion was still that: a crime scene. I had to keep that front of mind going in and look out for anything suspicious.

"Chris?" Griz asked, as she rolled down the window and hit the button on the intercom. "Is something on your mind?"

"Nope. I'm just hungry." I didn't like keeping secrets from Griselda, but she'd had a tough day at the Burger Bar, and it would only make her worry if I told her my suspicions about Nelly, her brother, and everyone else I'd run into this week.

"Good thing we're here, isn't it, dear?" Virginia asked.

"Don't worry, Watson," Missi said, gripping a bowl on her lap. "If Nelly's not prepared, we can always eat the salad."

"That's what's in the bowl?" I asked. "Salad?"

"Greek Salad." Missi lifted it, tapping fingers on the Saran wrap covering the top. "Don't you look at me like that, Watson. It's a delicious salad."

The gates swung open, and Grizzy steered the car up the drive before Missi could launch into a full verbal assault. Apparently, she was touchy about her salad, and if she was feeling on edge, the last thing I wanted to do was 'invoke the beast.'

We parked on the cobbled drive, next to a circular patch of garden—flowers I didn't recognize populating it —and clambered out of the car together.

"Would you look at this place," Griselda whispered, standing in front of the stone steps that led to the porch. If it could be called that.

Wraparound, caught between magnificent columns, and decorated with potted plants and two double swing-sets, the front of Nelly's house was more impressive than any place I'd lived in before.

"Somebody lucked out," Missi said.

"Oh, sister, don't talk like that. She's probably devastated about losing her mother."

"If she's devastated, then I'm Santa Claus' long lost cousin, Esmerelda," I said.

The three women looked at me.

"I'm just saying, she hasn't seemed overly unhappy about her mother's passing."

"Maybe it's the head injury," Grizzy said. "I heard about this one guy who got hit on the head in a car accident and afterward, he could see sounds."

"Seesaw?"

"No, see sounds. He saw sounds as colors and got really good at math," Grizzy said, nodding.

"Honey, how many times do I have to tell you?" Missi patted Griz on the shoulder with her free hand. "Don't believe everything you read on the internet."

"The one thing you can believe is that she's not unhappy about any of this," I whispered.

"Oh now, see, this is becoming awkward." Virginia

clicked her tongue. "We're hovering around outside gossiping about Nelly, and she's invited us for dinner. It's just wrong. We should be ashamed of ourselves."

Griselda grimaced. "You're right, Vee. Of course, you're right. We shouldn't—"

"—no idea!" The shout had come from inside the mansion. The massive dark wood doors stood open to greet us. Or perhaps, they were open because someone else had gone in before us.

"Was that Nelly?" Grizzy asked.

"No. Deeper voice." I moved up the steps, and the women followed me.

"—think you are?" Now, that had been Nelly. "You're not even my blood, not really."

"We're half-siblings," a young man replied. "That's the definition of blood, you idiot."

"Grayson," I said. "It's got to be Grayson."

Glass crashed inside, and Virginia hopped on the spot. "Oh my."

"Sounds like things are getting heated in there." Grizzy had gone pale.

There was only one thing for it. I marched into the entry hall and headed toward the shouts and tumult. I came out in a living room with parquet flooring, Persian carpets, and a chandelier overhead.

Nelly stood near a fireplace, grasping a picture frame to her chest. Glass lay shattered at her feet. "How dare you," she hissed. "How dare you ruin our mother's memory?"

"Our mother's memory?" Grayson stood nearer to the door, his fists balled at his sides. "You didn't even know her. You didn't even like her. She told me how you treated her when she first came to town, yet here you are, sharing the profits now that she's gone. It's not fair."

"Grow up." Nelly hadn't noticed me yet, and I remained dead still, observing. "What happened between me and mom is none of your business. What did you expect? I didn't know either of you. I didn't even believe you were real when I first met you."

"It's wrong. I had to spend my days working for my money, working to prove that I was worthy of an inheritance, and you meet her for a week, and, suddenly, you're in the will?" Grayson came forward, but didn't move past the glass coffee table. He pointed at Nelly. "I'm not going to let this happen. You're going to move out of this mansion, do you hear me?"

"Get out!" Nelly yelled. "Get out of my house."

"It's not your house." But Grayson stalked from the living room, casting a nasty look at me as he passed.

Nelly's face screwed up and tears streaked down her cheeks. She turned and kicked the fire poker's stand. The brass poker clanged and dropped to the floor.

"Nelly?" Was it safe to approach?

She turned, eyes widening. "Christie! Oh my gosh,

I'm so sorry you had to witness that. I-I can't believe that just happened." She lifted the picture from her chest and peered down at it, then turned and placed it on the mantel.

The frame had no glass, but the image was clear. A new photo with a glossy sheen—Nelly and her mother standing together, smiling at the camera. Martha had been Nelly's spitting image, with mousy brown hair and the same innocent eyes. Better fashion sense though. No droopy cardigan in sight.

I had so many questions and none of them were sympathetic. "Grizzy." I needed the cavalry to come in and sweep up the emotional pieces.

Griselda, Vee and Missi entered and flocked toward Nelly, immediately. They cooed and patted her on the back. Missi tried cheering her up with the news of her fantastic Greek Salad.

Finally, Nelly's eyes dried, though her cheeks remained a splotchy pink. "This is not how I imagined the start of our evening together. I had the chef prepare us a delicious meal, Salmon En Croute, and now this happens. I'm so sorry, you guys. I don't know what came over me. I shouldn't have lost my temper."

Truthfully, I'd never seen Nelly that angry before. She'd looked ready to grab the fire poker and assault her half-brother. I might've been reading too much into it.

"He's such a horrible little man," Nelly said, and her

eyes flashed. "I've never met anyone I didn't like until him. He's all greasy and mean, and you'd think he would've found what he wanted to do by now. He doesn't look it, but he's twenty-three-years-old. But no, he'd prefer to work in Sal's Pizzeria and live off my mother."

Twenty-three? Talk about stunted growth development.

"Sorry about this," I said, briskly.

Grizzy drew Nelly into another hug. "Let's try to forget about it. We can eat dinner and relax together, talk about happier things."

"Thanks, girls," Nelly said, and dried her eyes with the ends of her cardigan sleeves.

We progressed from the living room into a grand dining hall, which wouldn't have looked out of place in a palace, and took our seats at a long banquet table. Places had already been set for us at one end.

Missi plonked her ceramic bowl down between the crystal glasses and peeled off the cling film on top. "This should go well with the salmon," she said, stubbornly.

"Yeah, I've heard that about French and Greek foods," I replied.

She pointed a gnarled finger at me.

I shrugged it off. Nelly had already launched into the tale of how Grayson had come barging in to ruin her night. Every now and again, her jaw would clench, her nostrils flare.

I'd misjudged her. She did care about her mother's passing. That or she cared about the money.

Either way, Nelly and Grayson had both risen on my suspect list.

The meals came out, and we tucked in. The salmon was tender, pink and delicious, and the greens served with it were tasty, as well. I took some of Missi's Greek Salad, simply to avoid her wrath, and was pleasantly surprised by the flavor.

While the women chattered on, my thoughts took a turn.

This was the crime scene. Sure, it had been cleaned up, but it was still—

"—shot in the upstairs living room," Nelly said, and sniffed. "She fell right on the carpet in there. They removed it. Thankfully, there are no ... markings from what happened, but still. It's just terrible. Terrible. And I don't want to point any fingers, but I've got to say, the person who knocked me aside seemed quite skinny."

"Like Grayson?" Grizzy asked.

"Exactly. But like I said, I don't want to lay any blame. The police will figure it out. Or Christie." Nelly favored me with a smile.

I didn't trust it. "Where's the ladies' room?" I asked.

"Oh, there's one in the hall next to the stairs," Nelly said. "I can have Jeffrey show you if you like?"

"No, I can find it on my own, thanks." I got up from

the table and exited the room, trying to keep a straight face.

It was snooping time.

I made my way down the hall and to the stairs, my footsteps muffled by the thick carpets placed to accent the tapestries on the walls. I ignored the downstairs bathroom, placed my hand on the polished balustrade, and made my way up to the second floor.

Shot in the upstairs living room.

That was what Nelly had said. If I'd daydreamed any longer, I would have missed it. I had to stop doing that in company.

I reached the landing and looked left and right. Every inch of this place was fancier than the last. I started my search and, finally, found the upstairs living room. It would have been easier to ask Nelly to take a look around, but a part of me didn't want her to know.

She was a suspect, plain and simple. Though she had been knocked out by the killer, there was the off-chance that she'd planned that and had been working with an accomplice.

I stood in the center of the upstairs living room, the light on overhead, and turned in a circle. The floors were wooden and clean. Scratches on the floor near the sofas. Someone had pushed them out of position. Forensics team? Probably.

Bookcase had been moved too—some of the books

had dropped onto their sides or been placed back upside down. Shoddy work.

A Grand piano sat underneath a set of French windows, polished to a sheen. No scrapes on the floor near it, though it had wheels. It might have been moved.

"Shot where?" I muttered, and tried to place myself in the scene.

What would Martha have been doing in this room?

Playing the piano? A folder sat atop the stand attached to the front of it. Sheet music. And there was no TV. She might have been reading books, but there was dust on the spines of the ones that hadn't been moved.

Dust on the spines, but Martha had recently moved into the mansion. Perhaps, it had come furnished by the previous owner? Why hadn't the maids been up here to dust the shelves? House had been empty for a while? New staff?

I didn't sit on the velvet-topped stool in front of the Grand Piano, but stood behind it, my hands clasped at my back.

Sitting here, and then... killer enters.

I looked over my shoulder at the door, turning.

The killer has a gun and points it. Martha gets up. Why wouldn't she have gotten up? Confronted with a gun, would she have wilted against the piano? No, if that was the case, the piano would have been damaged by her falling on it.

Martha puts her hands up. She's shot and falls on the carpet.

I scanned the floor and caught the faint outline of a circle.

Carpet was removed.

I strode to the other side of the room and stood next to the sofa, surveying the scene from that side, but it was too far from the dark circle on the floor—clearly, the carpet hadn't been moved in a long time. If Martha had been on either of the sofas, it would have taken her extra time to leap up and get to the patch.

Either way, she had died on it. Could she have been standing randomly in the room, peering out the window? Possibly. But my gut directed me toward the Grand Piano.

Something was off about it. Or around it.

I moved to it, scooched around and scanned the dark polished sides.

Killer fired the gun. How many shots?

I didn't know. I didn't have any information on the actual crime, and it irked me. If I'd had one more clue...

A hole had punctured the side of the piano, and I studied it, opting not to touch. I tracked its trajectory through to the other side of the piano, then followed that line toward the window's sill. Just beneath it, a hole sat in the plaster.

Something metal glinted inside.

Good heavens, they missed it. How did they miss it?

But it was an obscure spot, and, without a ballistics expert around, it might have been an easy miss.

I had left my bag on the coat stand downstairs. I crept down to get it, the hum of talk from the dining hall a comfort—they weren't worried about my absence—and moved back upstairs. I extracted a tweezers and a trusty pack of Kleenex then removed the projectile from the plaster. It sprinkled dust beneath the window.

I deposited the bullet into the tissue and wrapped it up. There was no casing on the ground—they had found that, but not the projectile? Or had someone interfered with the scene before the police arrived?

Regardless, I had a hard evidence. Illegally, but still. It was something I could use to find out more about the murder weapon and the case.

"Christie?" Grizzy called from downstairs. I hurried to the door, tucking the bullet carefully into a side pocket of my purse.

❧ 8 ❧

"I shouldn't be doing this," Grizzy said, as she strode down the sidewalk at my side. "I should be in the Burger Bar, minding my own business. And you should give that bullet over to the cops, immediately. This is none of our business, Christie."

"See, now, when I agreed that you could come along, I meant you could do so if you didn't complain and tell me I'm sticking my nose where it doesn't belong." I sighed, my pace brisk as we headed toward the gun store in Sleepy Creek. "You see, I'm well aware of how dangerous this is. And how stubborn I am."

"As a mule," Grizzy muttered, but there was a spring in her step.

Whether Griz liked to admit it or not. She got excited about these investigations too. The look of horror she'd given me when we'd gotten back from

Nelly's mansion the night before had faded fast and been replaced by curiosity.

We entered a side street off Main, and found the gun shop with its dusty glass windows, gate at the entrance, and a glinting golden sign overhead that read 'Sleepy Creek's Guns Galore.'

I walked up to it and buzzed the button outside.

The gate clanked and admitted us into the warm and leather-scented store. A woman stood at the back, behind a thick glass topped counter. She leaned on it, paging idly through a magazine, and wore her hair bright pink and cropped short.

"Morning," I said, and walked up to her.

"And morning to you," the woman said. "Name's Candy."

I took her hand and shook it. "Christie, and this is Griselda."

Grizzy gave a timid wave. "Hi Candz."

"Griz."

"I wonder if you can help me with something," I said.

"Sure can do," Candy replied, straightening and dusting off her studded jacket. "If what you need help with is guns, of course."

"It is." There was no point whipping out the bullet I'd removed from the plaster at Nelly's new mansion. It was deformed, and identifying a bullet without its casing was nearly impossible without the murder weapon. It was clear it hadn't come from a shotgun, though. No pellets or scatter. That left rifles and handguns. I would have to hand the evidence over soon, but not before I had the information I needed.

"Then fire away," Candy said. "Excuse the pun."

"I was wondering if you'd sold a handgun recently," I replied.

Candy blinked. It was an ambiguous question. I didn't blame her. "Recently? You know what type of gun you're looking for?"

"No," I said.

"Are you a police officer?" Candy asked.

"No."

"She's a detective from Boston," Grizzy put in. "But she's not technically on duty."

"Sure, sure. Just, it's a strange question to ask in light of what happened recently. I've already had the cops come in here asking question about Martha Boggs, and now you're asking…"

I nodded, but kept my lips together. She could choose to help me or out me.

"Look, I know who you are," Candy said. "You're the detective who solved Franny's case. Franny was a good friend of mine."

"I didn't technically solve it on my own."

"Oh, that's not what I heard," Candy said. "Gossip on the streets says that you got to the bottom of it, and without your help, the police wouldn't have solved the case."

"No," I said. "The police here are good at their jobs." And it was true. I just happened to be working in a way that was quicker and easier because sticking within the confines of warrants and the law hadn't been my M.O.

Thankfully, the extent of my law-breaking had yet to be discovered. If it had been, the sparse evidence I had collected wouldn't be permissible in court.

"I'm not saying they aren't good at their jobs." Candy offered me a gap-toothed smile. "But, they don't get results as fast as you do."

I'd take it as a compliment. "That mean you'll help me?"

"Give me a second." She disappeared through a doorway behind the counter.

"Let's hope she's not calling Liam," I said.

"Don't be so negative. She wants to help."

"Now who's excited about partaking in an investigation?" I nudged my friend, and Grizzy gave a sheepish grin.

Candy returned carrying a thick ledger and plopped it down on top of the counter. She paged through it, scanning lines of names and numbers. "Here we go," she said, and pressed her finger to a row. "These are the sales I made for the last few weeks leading up to the murder."

"You don't keep electronic files?" I asked.

"Why does everyone keep asking me that? I don't like computers. Never have trusted them. My sister's an author and she told me that she once lost an entire manuscript because her file thingy didn't back up properly. No thank you."

"Right." I leaned in. "You were saying?"

"I've only made a few sales in the past week. I'll read them out to you," she said. "Glock 43, purchased by Nelly Boggs and Mark Donovan. Smith and Wesson—"

"Whoa, whoa, wait, can you repeat that, please?"

"Sure." Candy cleared her throat. "Glock 43, purchased by Nelly Boggs and Mark Donovan. They're a couple, came in here smiling and holding hands like they were buying an engagement ring instead of a nine mill."

I exchanged a glance with Grizzy.

"Any other names?"

"Mmm, yeah." She rattled them off, but none of them rang a bell or, if they did, they belonged to folks we knew were serious about home security, like Mrs. Immelmann across the street. I could easily take the short list and run through alibis. I noted the names down, but two stuck in the forefront of my mind.

Nelly and Donovan. Why would they have bought a gun and so soon before Martha's death?

This only compounded my suspicion that Nelly might have worked with someone else.

"Anything else you need from me, just holler," Candy

said. "I'm happy to do favors for upstanding Sleepy Creekers like you, Miss Watson. You helped bring justice to Franny's killer. I'm eternally grateful for that. She went to high school with me, you know. Great girl."

We thanked Candy and walked through the store and toward the exit. She buzzed us out.

I stepped onto the sidewalk and nearly ran over a pole of a man, wearing a wispy mustache and a glittering gold watch.

He stumbled. "Oh my!"

"Sorry," I called out, and caught his arms. "I didn't see you there."

"Learn to watch where you're going." He ripped himself free of me and marched off down the street, grunting and growling under his breath.

"Is it just me, or are the folks in Sleepy Creek getting friendlier?" I asked.

"Don't worry about Mr. Huxley, Chris. He's always been a crotchety old dude," Grizzy said.

"Mr. Huxley? Wait, that's Janine's father?"

"Yeah, why?"

"No reason." But I watched the elderly gentleman turn the corner and stride out of sight. Janine's dad. Could he have been connected to the crime somehow? Or was I just grasping at straws here, after all, there was no evidence that Janine was involved, either.

Besides, I had more important matters to take care

off, now. Namely, the fact that Nelly had had a gun and hadn't disclosed that information to me. If she'd been serious about me investigating, that was important.

Why would she have hidden it from me? Surely, she had to realize that her owning a firearm would make her suspicious, given that she'd benefitted directly from Martha's death.

"Chris?"

"Hmm?"

"You're staring into space again." Grizzy waved her hand in front of my face. "What's up?"

"I need to talk to Nelly."

"It will have to wait until after your shift at the restaurant," Grizzy said, and checked her watch. "If we don't get back soon, poor Hedy and Martin will be overrun by customers. Look, it's almost time for the lunch rush."

"Duly noted." I followed Griz toward the Burger Bar. Not even burgers could dampen my desire to get to the bottom of it.

The closer I got to the truth, the clearer the picture became, and it was starting to look a lot like the doe-eyed florist, Nelly.

After the lunch rush, I excused myself from the restaurant to snack on one of the Breakfast Burgers Jarvis had whipped up. Ironically, we served it at all hours of the day. It was a stroke of marketing genius on Grizzy's part, and a taste explosion on the chef's.

I seated myself on a bench outside the restaurant and bit into my burger. The flavors and textures combined, perfectly. The savory of the meat, the creaminess of the egg yolk, and the crisp tartness of the fresh sliced tomato.

I shut my eyes and relished the moment, cars humming by in Main Street.

The lunch rush had been so busy, I'd barely had time to contemplate the gun purchase. Or the fact that Nelly hadn't introduced us to her boyfriend. Was there a reason for that? Perhaps, a choice to hide him from her friends?

Friends.

I'd always been fascinated by the mindset of a killer. Sure, there was passion and rage and jealousy, but how could someone lack so much empathy they could take another's life? Could kind little Nelly really have done that to her own mother? Granted, the mother who abandoned her as a child?

Anything's possible.

I'd learned as much in Boston and Sleepy Creek.

I opened my eyes and took another bite of my burger, my taste buds transported to heaven, but my gaze fixed on the florist's shop across the street. It was open, and I could barely make out the silhouette of Nelly behind the counter.

I've got to do it now. Get it out of the way. If she cares about finding out who killed her mother, she won't take offense.

A man, tall and broad-shouldered, with ginger hair, strode down the sidewalk opposite. His hands were tucked into the pockets of his jeans, and he whistled a tune, loudly. He stopped in front of the florist's, slicked his hair back then entered.

I put my burger in its box, lifted my napkin and dabbed.

Now, who was that?

I'd stayed in Sleepy Creek a while, and sure, I didn't

know everyone, but I'd gotten used to the faces around here, and I'd never seen this guy around. Could he be the guy Nelly was dating? And if so, what on earth was he so happy about?

I closed my box, got up, and hurried across the street. I'd been meaning to speak to Nelly about what had happened, and now seemed the perfect time. Especially if it got me a glimpse into who the boyfriend was.

The bell above the door tinkled as I entered the shop.

Nelly leaned over the counter, her palms tucked beneath her chin, making eyes at the new guy. He grinned at her in turn.

"Hi," I said.

"Oh, Christie!" Nelly straightened, a dreamy smile on her face.

The guy turned toward me. Freckles across his nose up close, ice blue eyes, and stubble along his chin. He stuck out his hand. "Nice to meet you. Nelly's told me about you and your friend Griselda. Name's Donovan. Donovan Marks."

I shook his hand. "You already know my name," I said.

"Sure do. Your reputation precedes you in this town. The big Boston detective."

"Sure. Without the 'big' part."

Nelly laughed, a sound that was nothing like her

normal chuckle. She kept staring at Donovan like he was Santa Claus or something. Or a magical fairy that would grant her a wish.

Maybe I was being cynical, but I'd never felt like that about anyone before.

"You work at the Burger Bar, yeah?" Donovan asked.

He had a strange accent I couldn't quite place, like a mixture of different places. I didn't like that—I was usually pretty good at identifying people and their habits, but this guy was neat. No ketchup stains or wrinkles. As far as I could tell, he cared about his appearance, and that was it.

"Yeah," I said, slowly, gesturing with the box in my hand. "I'm on my lunch break. Thought I'd come by for a chat with Nelly."

"Oh, that's wonderful," Nelly said. "I'm always happy to chat, but I did want to spend some time with Donovan."

"That's OK." The boyfriend waved a hand. "I've got the whole day free, Nels. I can hang around for a while." He glanced at me. "See, I moved to town a week ago. I'm living next door to you, actually, on the right side?"

"Huh?" I blinked. We had Ray Tolentino on the right, depending on which way you looked at it.

"Or the left. Ha, depending on which way you look at it."

Creepy. "I had no idea anyone had moved out," I said.

But then, I was mostly at the Burger Bar or walking Curly Fries or chatting with the terrible twins. "Welcome to the neighborhood, I guess."

"Yeah, thanks."

That made this even more awkward. I cleared my throat. "Nelly, perhaps it would be best if I spoke to you in private. I have a question for you, regarding... Martha."

"It's fine, Chris. Anything you need to say, you can say in front of Donovan. I tell him everything." She fluttered her eyelashes at him. He rounded the counter and slipped his arm around her waist, pulling her closer.

I wasn't the most professional waitress in town, but I did draw the line at public displays of affection. It seemed inappropriate. I hadn't found the reason for that type of thing yet. I couldn't picture any circumstances under which I'd cuddle Liam in public.

Don't you dare think about him now. Focus. The gun.

"Why didn't you tell me you bought a gun a week before your mother was shot?" Boy, I'd never been good at mincing my words. "You want me to check out what's going on around town, but you omitted information. Why?"

Nelly grew pale. Donovan blinked as if he couldn't quite register what I'd asked.

"Well?"

"I—It was a gift," Nelly said. "Donovan was worried about me living in Sleepy Creek, what with all the murders going on, so he bought me the gun as a gift. Are you accusing me of something?"

"Everyone's a suspect," I replied. "I have to follow the leads. You realize how suspicious this looks. You two buying a weapon together, Martha dying, and you being the benefactor of the estate."

"I didn't do anything wrong." Nelly's eyebrows drew downward. "I didn't. I didn't even have the gun with me on the day of the—I don't know how it wound up being used by the killer."

My eyebrows lifted. "Your gun is the murder weapon."

"I think it's time you leave," Donovan said.

Nelly hugged Donovan and buried her face in his shirt, her shoulders shaking.

"Now. And don't come back."

"Fine," I said. "I'll leave. But you can bet that I *will* get to the bottom of this. That's what Nelly asked me to do, and that's what's going to happen." I didn't like that I'd hurt Nelly's feelings, but she hadn't been honest with me from the start.

I left the florist's and, possibly, my friendship with Nelly behind, frustration and guilt gathering in my gut.

❧ 10 ❧

Grizzy had taken the late shift at the Burger Bar, and I had the evening to myself to mull over the murder weapon, Nelly, and my new next door neighbor. The mind boggled at how he'd sneaked in under the radar, but there it was.

I stood in the living room, the curtains on the side window drawn back, and watched the fence that separated Grizzy's home from the one next door. The lights were on, but I couldn't make out any movement.

"Hmmm." What if Donovan and Nelly had acted as accomplices to take down Martha?

It seemed unthinkable. Nelly had been nothing but a sweetheart since I'd first moved to Sleepy Creek, but then, she might have been acting all along. Involved in the murders. What if she was a Spider?

"Now, you're being ridiculous." I took a breath and let the curtain fall back into place. "Maybe the pressure of this is getting to me. Am I losing my touch?" I was talking to myself again. So that had to mean something.

I turned and found Curly Fries seated directly in my path to the kitchen, her yellow eyes ghoulish among the black fur.

"What?" I asked.

She meowed and flicked her tail.

"You had better not be asking me for food. It's still fifteen minutes until feeding time," I said. "You know the rules, cat. I feed you early, Grizzy gets angry with me, and we both have to go on an extra walk tomorrow. Play fair."

She meowed again.

"It's for your own good. Look at you. You're already getting slimmer and healthier." This was partly because we'd taken a plate of cookies over to Mrs. Immelmann across the road and begged her to stop feeding Curly.

She'd called us two days ago and let us know that Curly had thrown the cat version of a tantrum upon realizing that Mrs. Immelmann wouldn't feed her anymore. She'd scratched up her window sill, gone number two in the flower bed, and killed a bird in protest.

"Sometimes, I think you're too smart for your own good," I said.

Curly gave a low growl.

I ignored it and walked past, heading for the kitchen. She batted my legs then followed me, a purr starting up in her kitty throat.

"Is that what you think?" She wound between my ankles. "It's still not time. See?" I pointed to the clock above the counter.

I set about making coffee, occasionally tripping over Curly, muttering under my breath.

The murder weapon belonged to Nelly. Yet they hadn't arrested her. They would know it was hers, and that meant they didn't have enough evidence to put her away. Perhaps, Nelly had had a solid alibi leading up to the moment when she was struck over the head? Or they had no fingerprints. It could be, that Nelly's gun had been kept in a safe at the mansion, and that—

A knock rattled the front door, and I paused, holding my mug. It was upside down. Whoever the visitor was, they'd saved me from pouring coffee onto the bottom of my cup rather than into it.

Another volley of banging knocks.

"Just a moment!" I called out, and put my cup down the right way up.

Curly meowed, but stayed put.

I headed to the front door and opened it.

Liam stood on the doorstep wearing his uniform and a frown.

"Uh oh," I said.

"Uh oh, indeed. May I come in?"

"Of course." I led him through to the kitchen, a sinking feeling in the pit of my stomach. "Can I get you something to eat? A cup of coffee?"

"Coffee's fine," he said. "Thanks.'

I poured two mugs, brought them to the table, and set out the cream and sugar.

Liam accepted the coffee but didn't take a sip. "Why did you accuse Nelly Boggs of murder this afternoon?"

"I didn't," I replied. "I merely asked why she hadn't told me that she had bought a gun a week before her mother was shot."

Liam groaned and pinched the bridge of his nose. "Oh, Christie."

"What? I know I'm not the best with, uh, emotional conversations, but it seemed the appropriate thing to ask."

"Firstly, no, that's not appropriate at all. And secondly, you aren't supposed to be getting involved. You're making this incredibly difficult for me. I've cut you a break several times, and now, things are even more complicated. We've been on a date together."

I swallowed. "Hold on. Before you reprimand me for doing the wrong thing, you should know... Just wait here." I got up and hurried through to the living room where I'd dropped my bag on the table. I withdrew the

Kleenex from the side pocket and walked it over to Liam.

"What's this?" he asked.

"A projectile I found at the crime scene."

"What?!"

"Behind the piano, underneath the window sill. Clean shot through. I don't know what that means for your case or why it wasn't found during the initial sweep of the scene, but there it is. I've been meaning to give it to you."

"Tell me you didn't break into Nelly's house to get this."

I sighed. "We were invited over for dinner."

Liam shut his eyes. "That means there was more than one shot fired," he said. "We'll have to look at the scene again."

"I found it and handed it in. That's got to count for something."

"It counts for you getting in a whole mess of trouble if you don't back off. I'm done giving second chances, Christie. This is for your own good."

"Look," I said, and paused to take a sip of my coffee for strength and courage. "You and I both know that that's never going to happen. I mentioned to you in the past that I'll take the consequences that come. Liam, when I arrived in Sleepy Creek, I wanted to get back to Boston and keep my nose clean. Now, I want to figure out what's going on here, even if that costs me my job or lands my in jail for interfering. I don't expect you to do your job any different. I just... I'm trying to do the right thing."

He didn't say anything.

"And the fact is, this case reminds me of my mother's in a way. Nelly's mom died. She needs help solving it. And I guess I'm too over-enthusiastic.'

Liam turned his coffee mug in a circle on the kitchen table. "I don't expect you to change who you are, Christie. Just don't do anything illegal to get results. If you want to gossip or chat with people I won't do anything to stop it, but I draw the line at removing evidence from a crime scene. I'm letting it slide, now, but next time, call me. Call me first."

It was as good as permission as I could get from him. "Thank you," I said.

"And I think it's best if we don't go on another date until after this case has been solved."

"Agreed."

Liam rose from the table. "Then I'll get going. I've got to get this evidence back and check out the scene again. Though, at this point it's clear the evidence may have been tampered with." He gave me a quick smile, one that set free the butterflies in my belly, then left the kitchen. The door clicked shut a moment later.

And that was it. I had my suspicions, and all I could

do now was poke and prod and hope I didn't cross the line.

Curly Fries meowed at me from next to her kibble bowl.

"All right," I said, "now it's time to eat."

‮‮
❧ 11 ❧

"You're seriously going to stay out of it?" Grizzy asked, as she whipped me up my malt choc shake for my brunch time break.

The restaurant had grown quiet after the morning rush, as per usual, but I wasn't as happy about it as I usually would have been. When I was busy, I didn't have a chance to obsess over the case.

"I'm going to do what I normally do, but try not to get in Liam's way this time. Or do anything illegal."

"Let's see if that pans out."

"You don't have full faith in me? I'm shocked." It was sarcasm, of course. I wouldn't blame Griselda for doubting me. In the short time I'd lived in Sleepy Creek, I'd broken into bakeries and personal homes. I'd snooped and invaded crime scenes. I'd solved cases too. My track record spoke for itself.

Grizzy finished up the shake by plopping some whipped cream on top and adding a cherry.

I lifted it by the reddened stem and deposited it into my mouth, crunching on the sugary sweetness. It was some solace, at least. "I want to get to the bottom of it," I said.

"I know, you and the quest for truth." Grizzy waved hand. "But you'll be on a quest to get out of prison if you don't stick to your promises this time around."

"No, not a quest for truth. I want to help keep Sleepy Creek safe too."

"Did I hear you right?" Grizzy asked. "Are you saying that you ... like it here?"

"Keep your voice down." I poked the milkshake with my straw. "If Missi hears you, she'll tease me endlessly."

The twins were seated at their usual corner booth, Missi with the newspaper pressed flat in front of her, tapped her fingernails against a half-full milkshake glass. Virginia held an iPad and scrolled, her reading glasses perched on the end of her nose. They'd both had their burgers. Missi had done her morning flirting with Jarvis, as well.

"All right, so what are you going to—?"

The front door slapped open, the bell tinkling so fast it trilled, and Mona Jonah clomped into the restaurant. I watched her in the mirror behind the counter.

She ripped pink sunglasses from her face and glared around.

Missi grimaced at her.

Mona lifted two fingers and placed them underneath her eyes then pointed at the terrible twin.

"Yeah? And so, what are you going to do about it?" Missi growled in response.

"You want to start something you can't finish, old woman?"

"Old woman! I look younger than you!" Missi struggled upright.

Virginia gave a long-suffering sigh.

"Ladies," Grizzy called, in her sing-song voice. "Let's keep it calm, please. The restaurant is big enough for both of you to share. Mona? Can I get you something?"

The yellow-haired maven of gossip stomped up to the counter and dumped her garish leopard-print tote on it. She took a seat next to me, the stool squeaking a complaint, and huffed out a breath. "Hit me with a double malt banana, extra cream, extra cherries."

"I volunteer to do the hitting," Missi called.

Mona, to her credit, ignored the jibe. "And give me one of those Breakfast Burgers too. Nothing makes me hungrier than unbridled rage." She grasped the straps of her handbag and squeezed like she could choke them to death.

"What happened?" I asked, spinning on my stool to

lean my elbows on the bar and face the dining area in case my tables needed me.

"Family," she grunted.

Mona wasn't usually so forthcoming without first insulting either me or Grizzy or the restaurant or all three. She had to be seriously irritated if she could get past her usual mean streak.

"Oh?"

"I will never understand how people think," Mona continued. "Never. I am a kind, giving person, wouldn't you say?"

Missi snorted loudly.

"When Richard and that torrid little creature he calls his offspring decided to sell their mansion and needed a place to stay while the purchase of their next home was finalized, what did I say?"

"Yes?" I suggested.

"Yes. That's exactly what I said. I opened my home to them. I told them they were more than welcome to live with me, as long as they paid for some food and utilities. Richard assured me that they would live by my rules. That they would stay quiet at certain hours, particularly after bed time."

The diatribe was so fascinating, heads around the restaurant turned to observe. It was like witnessing a building being demolished.

Mona reached up and poke a dark half circle under

one eye. "Look at me! Look at the state of me! I can't possibly maintain the Gossip Circle and the editing of the paper and the new Council for Proper Usage of Lawn Ornaments in this state. It's a crime, I tell you. If they weren't my family, I would report them."

Griselda drowned out the last of Mona's sentence by turning the blender on for the milkshake. After, she poured it into a glass and did a double scoop of whipped cream and two cherries as requested. She slid the shake over the counter, and Mona attacked it.

She slurped and chewed and prodded with a dessert spoon.

"What did they do?" I asked.

Everyone in the restaurant was curious. The show had to go on.

"What didn't they do? That Richard is never home and when he is, he's just ... oh, he just sits around and expects to be waited on hand and foot. Like I'm his maid." She spat a little mashed up cherry onto the counter. "And that daughter of his. Do not *even* get me started."

I turned, whipped my handy rag from the front pocket of my apron and wiped away the mess on the counter. "Oh, but we do want to get you started. I mean, it's important you get it out?"

Grizzy nodded. "Christie's right. If you keep all the anger in, it will only hurt you."

"Or her next victim," Missi called out.

"Janine." Mona plumbed the depths of her milkshake with the straw. "Janine is the worst excuse for a young lady I have ever encountered in my life. Always out late, comes home in the dead of the night and plays music in the living room at a screamingly loud decibel level. I can't take it anymore. I can't take it, I tell you. I haven't slept properly in over a week." Mona reached up and tugged furiously on her golden hoop earring. "Unbelievable."

"I'm sorry to hear that, Mona," Grizzy said. "But surely, they won't be staying with you for much longer."

"Who knows?" Mona asked. "Knowing my luck, those two idiots will be around for the next month."

Jarvis rang the bell in the kitchen window. "Order up, mon," he called.

Grizzy delivered Mona's burger to the table, and she tucked into it. The burgers at the restaurant were so good, they could stop a raging Mona in her tracks. We had to put that on the menu somewhere.

The Huxley living situation tickled at the back of my mind. They had lived in Martha's mansion, and Janine was involved, somehow, with Grayson Boggs. What was the connection?

If I could find it... but no, gossiping was one thing. Liam had specifically asked me not to get involved by doing anything drastic. I'd try to play by his rules, for now.

Still, the question marks drifted through my mind as I waited my tables.

12

The scent of bubbling cheese, cooking noodles, and the savory tang of tomato-beef lasagna filled Griselda's kitchen. I inhaled it from where I stood at the kitchen counter, doing the unthinkable.

Chopping vegetables. Griselda had managed to enlist my help in preparing the food. Now, I was all for making coffee or paying for a pizza, even for waiting on tables, but I knew my strengths. They didn't lie in cooking.

"Am I doing this right?" I asked.

"Yes, of course. Why wouldn't you be? C'mon, Chris, you're just slicing up some tomatoes. It's not like it's rocket science."

"No, but it's culinary science. Cooking is like science, you know. I read that somewhere once. I remember laughing about it, but now, I get it. Hard work, great reward, total precision." I sliced a piece of tomato onto the chopping board. "This might be my new calling."

"I'll tell Jarvis that next time he needs to chop onions for the burgers."

"Don't you dare."

Grizzy laughed from her position in front of the oven. She would bend every now and again and check how the lasagna was doing, then straighten and take a sip of her diet soda. Her hawk eyes ensured I didn't mess up too badly.

"You know, I've been thinking," she said.

Hopefully, it wasn't about the case. I'd been obsessing over it all day, and I didn't need the extra nudge to get back to it. The tomatoes had finally distracted me. *Poor Martha. Not that I knew her or anything, but still. Shot down after she'd bought an exceptionally expensive mansion and started reconnecting with her kids.*

"Chris?"

"Hmm, yeah?"

"I said I've been thinking."

"This is a good thing. Not thinking leads to dangerous accidents."

Grizzy took another sip of soda. "We haven't properly celebrated your birthday yet."

I finished slicing the tomatoes and scooped the pieces into a salad bowl, on top of already washed and torn fresh lettuce. "We have. You got me that awesome

Poirot book, and I had a burger in bed while Curly stared at me." I still hadn't told her that I'd fed Curly a bit of meat. That was our little secret, and a lapse in judgment on my part. Now, I wasn't sure if the stares from the cat had murderous intent, or she simply expected me to produce another burger out of my back pocket and start feeding her mince chunks.

"No, that's not enough. I've been thinking we should go somewhere."

"Like where?" I asked.

"I don't know, but I'm going to figure it out. I'll keep it a surprise. Just as long as I know that you're up for it?"

"Of course. I mean, I've never celebrated my birthday apart from when I was a kid and my mom threw parties," I said, and swallowed. It was still tough to talk about her at times. "But yeah, as an adult, I've never done that type of thing. I've never had any friends apart from you. Wow, that sounds pathetic."

"It's not pathetic, Christie. You're just a prickly person. Prickly people struggle to make friends, but they usually have the softest, wateriest centers. They're the best people to get to know."

"That was a prolonged cactus metaphor," I said, pointing the knife at her. "But I appreciate it."

"Don't wave that thing around. Knowing Sleepy Creek's luck, you'll end up accidentally slicing me instead of the ingredients."

"Speaking of which," I said, putting the knife down and eyeing it. "What's next? For the salad?"

"I'm thinking olives."

"Are we making Missi's not-Greek Salad?"

"Don't let her hear you say that." Grizzy headed for the fridge and brought out a jar of olives, then returned. "Already pitted." She put them down. "Slice them in half and put them in. About ten."

"A woman's work never ends." I spooned the olives out.

Grizzy fell into quiet and drank her soda. Curly Fries wandered into the kitchen and sat in the corner, silently. She didn't meow because she'd already had her kibble, but her eyes were set on the oven. She'd wind between the table legs while we ate, hoping for falling scraps of mince or cheese.

Sometimes, just to pay her back for always sleeping on my head, I'd drop a bit of tomato instead and inwardly chuckle at how she turned up her nose and stalked off. Worked like a charm.

The buzzer on the oven rang, and Griselda slipped on her oven mitts, bent and removed the dish. She set it on the counter top, the cheese golden-brown and bubbling.

"That smells divine."

"The sooner you finish the salad, the sooner we get to eat. It has to rest now, anyway, or we'll burn the roofs of our mouths."

Grizzy directed me the rest of the way on the salad then showed me how to whip up a simple olive oil and balsamic vinegar dressing. In no time, the food was ready and dished up. My knife and fork were seconds from carving into the dish when the phone rang.

I groaned. "It's probably just a telemarketer."

"I have to get it."

I snuck a bite of lasagna while Grizzy jumped up and was instantly transported to culinary heaven.

"Hello?" Grizzy answered the kitchen phone, twirling her finger through the cord. "Oh, hi Nelly. How are you?"

I looked up, the fork stalling halfway to my mouth. Grizzy had heard what had happened between Nelly and myself, and it had been a full day since we'd seen her. She hadn't even come into the restaurant for her usual lunch time treat.

"Yes, of course. No, not at all. I'm sure she wouldn't say no to that. Listen, Nelly, you don't have to worry about—Sure. OK, then, see you in a little while." Grizzy hung up.

"She's coming here?" I asked, putting my fork down.

"No. We're going there."

"Why?"

"Nelly wanted us to catch up, and also, she said she's worried."

"About what?" I asked, a mingling of curiosity at what Nelly wanted, and horror at the fact that I would have to stop eating this amazing food, took place inside me.

"She said she feels like she's being watched. Which is obviously concerning given what happened in that house." Grizzy shrugged, moved toward the table and lifted my plate off it, fork, knife and all. "Maybe she's just feeling paranoid."

"Or maybe not," I said, intrigued.

"I'm going to bag these up for us," Griz said. "Let's pack some overnight bags and head over there. We can share our meal with her."

"You really are too hospitable," I said. "How do you know I won't finish that whole lasagna by myself? Or that she won't feed us salmon again?"

"That salmon was nice. Sorry, some of us actually ate it instead of peeling bullets out of walls."

"Point taken." I got up from the table and moved off to collect my things and a book for the night. But I got the feeling I wouldn't be doing that much reading tonight, especially if there was someone 'watching' Nelly.

13

I'd already piled my overnight bag into the small trunk of Grizzy's Kia. She was inside quibbling over what to pack and trying to get Curly Fries into her kitty carrier. Judging by the last experience we'd had doing it, this would take a while.

I sat on the front step, my back to one of the wooden columns, and my nose tilted to the air, inhaling the scents of Sleepy Creek suburbia.

The sun had set a while ago, the dusk had come and gone. Lights were on in the front windows of houses, the smell of home cooking drifting around, sometimes shifted and replaced by the floweriness of a rose bed on the breeze. The leaves in Grizzy's maple tree rustled and whispered.

Crickets chirped, and I smiled. There was something

to be said for small town living. I'd sworn I'd never come back to it as an adult, but I couldn't deny how much I'd missed the relative peace and quiet in moments like these.

If this hadn't been murder capital, right now, I would have let the sleepiness take hold of me. But no, I forced myself to sit straighter, to be more alert.

A door slammed in the house next door, and a figure emerged.

Ginger hair. Tall and broad-shouldered. It was our new neighbor. Nelly's boyfriend—Donovan.

Interesting that she hadn't called him when she was afraid. Then again, it wasn't exactly proper for her to be calling an unmarried guy over to her house at night. If anything would start a nuclear gossip explosion, it was that. Mona Jonah would spontaneously arm like a submarine.

Donovan walked down his front path toward the mailbox, then opened it and rustled around inside. The walls between Grizzy's house and his were lower on the right side. His garden was pretty well kept, not exactly flower-filled or decorated, certainly not winning the council's award for most aesthetically pleasing lot.

"Evening," I called out.

Donovan zeroed in on me with his gaze. "Didn't see you there."

"Sorry, didn't mean to scare you."

"You didn't." He tucked his mail under his arm and came toward the fence that separated the properties.

I got up too and walked over, tucking my hands into the pockets of my jeans. "That's good to hear. It's not done in Sleepy Creek."

"What isn't?"

"Scaring your neighbors."

"But killing them is?" Donovan asked.

"You accusing me of something?"

"Just referring to the craziness in this town," he said, shrugging his shoulders. "So crazy that friends ask each other questions about guns and—"

"What happened in the florist's, well, Donovan, that's between Nelly and me. We'll sort it out," I said.

"She's my girlfriend. I'm going to protect her. I'm not going to let—"

I raised a palm. "I appreciate that, but Nelly and I have known each other for a while longer than you've known her."

"Like a week," he said.

He had a point. It wasn't like I'd been besties with Nelly for years. Still, the awkward vibe drifting between us had to go if I wanted to figure out exactly what Donovan was up to in town. Why he'd bought Nelly a gun in the first place. Why he had moved to Sleepy Creek.

Donovan cleared his throat. "I guess I'll go—"

"No, no, I'm sorry." I stuck out my hand. "Let's start over. Pretend we've just met as neighbors. That kind of thing's important in this town."

"Yeah, I've noticed." He shook my hand, and his shoulders eased a little bit. He had a splotch of something red on his shirt. Possibly leftovers from his dinner? Why was he eating alone? Why not with Nelly?

"How are you doing?" I asked. "Settling into the town well?"

"I guess you could say that," he replied. "Apart from living in this big house by myself."

"Looking for a roommate?" I asked.

"Definitely. One or two in fact," he said. "It's not like what I do covers all the expenses. I'm just counting on the finishing bonus from my last job covering me for the month."

"Oh? What do you do for a living?" I asked.

"I work in retail. I was transferred here from Logan's Rest. See, they've got a new department store opening here soon, and I'm going to be on the team." He puffed out his chest.

"A department store? That's a big move for this town."

"Big move for me too. Just glad I met Nelly to help me get by," he said, but his expression grew dark. "I just hate seeing what's going on with her."

"The murder?"

He nodded, glumly. "And the way she lets people take advantage of her good nature."

"What do you mean?"

"She's such a kind soul," he said. "But she's always willing to give, give, give when she should look after herself instead. She keeps helping that good for nothing brother of hers, even though he treats her like trash."

That was a strong way of putting it.

"Just the other day," he said, "I went over to visit her and found him there, lazing around on the sofa. He'd made a huge mess of the place and wouldn't clean up after himself. Said the maid could get it. Worse than that, he's pushing Nelly to sell. He wants his share of the money to go do whatever it is that men like him do. You seen what the guy wears?"

I nodded.

"All black, with that stringy hair. Excuse for a human if you ask me."

Now, that was a bit over the top.

"But Nelly still wants to help him. Other day when I got there? This dude's work vehicle had broken down, and he couldn't go out and deliver pizzas because of it," Donovan said. "I was the one who had to help him out. Trust me, the last thing I wanted to do was spend the rest of my night, that I planned on spending at dinner with my girlfriend, driving around in the car with that greaser."

"Sorry about that," I said, and glanced over my shoulder at the front of the house.

Grizzy hadn't emerged yet, but I needed an out. It was one thing to do some gossiping, but this dude was on a roll, and I had suddenly become his personal therapist.

"Can't believe I let him take advantage of me like that. It grinds my gears. Nelly's all sweet and nice, but that's not me. I don't let people walk all over me."

That would explain the gun-buying.

"And I don't let people hurt the folks I care about," he said.

"Well, I'm sorry to—"

"And when we were on our evening together, him stinking up the car with hair gel and that weird cologne he wears, and earrings! Earrings, for Pete's sake. He was so unprofessional. At one point, he stopped at someone's house just for a 'chat.' I had to threaten him to get him back in the car."

I perked up but tried not to make it obvious. "Oh yeah? Which house did you stop at?"

"I don't know the guy's name. He was some tall guy with gray hair. They had an argument in the front yard that drew people out onto the street to stare and point." Donovan shuddered at the humiliation.

Tall and gray hair. Not exactly defining features, but

could it have been Mr. Richard Huxley? "What were they arguing about?"

"I tried not to overhear. Why should I care about what that greaseball does or says?" Donovan paused. "But I think it was to do with a girl. He mentioned 'Janine' several times, and every time he did, the tall guy got increasingly frustrated. Eventually, the idiot came back to the car and got in, and I had to take him back to the restaurant to get his next order."

So, definitely Mr. Huxley then. What were they arguing about? Huxley clearly didn't want Grayson near his daughter. Or, perhaps, it had been more involved than that?

The front door clapped behind me, and I nearly jumped. Grizzy had finally appeared, carrying her bag and Curly's carrier. Black kitty paws peeked out of the gate and swatted at the air. Curly hated being in the carrier, even though it was state-of-the-art as cat carriers went.

"There," Grizzy called. "Ready."

I went over to help her with the bags, opting not to get myself scratched by raging Curly Fries.

"Who were you talking to?" she asked, nodding toward the fence.

Donovan had already headed back inside. He'd had his cathartic moment and called it quits right after.

"The new neighbor," I said, and left it at that.

I already had new information to digest. Huxley and Grayson knew each other. Was it possible Huxley wanted the Boggs boy to stay away from Janine out of fear for her life?

$$\text{※ } 14 \text{ ※}$$

"Thanks for coming," Nelly said, and opened the door of her grand mansion for us. She wore her same old cardigan and glasses, but her hair had been done up on top of her head. It was a giant, leaning tower of curls.

"You look lovely," Grizzy said.

I held back my opinion. Nelly was a sweetheart, but the curls didn't do her justice. Also, they made her look ready to topple over.

"Thank you." Nelly stepped back, and we entered, our footsteps echoing in the vast entry hall. "You know, I've just been so upset about what happened, Christie. We're friends, and I think I overreacted the last time we spoke."

I paused. "Nelly, I understand why you were upset."

"No, no, it's fine. There's no need to apologize or

anything like that. I think we should just put it behind us. Water under the bridge?"

"Sure," I replied, though I wouldn't be putting my suspicions behind us, under the bridge or anywhere else. "You mentioned being afraid?"

"Yes." Nelly shut the door and latched it, hastily. "I don't know what it is, but I keep hearing noises in the house, and I know that Grayson isn't here. Neither are Milly and Roger."

"And they are?" I asked, as we carried the foil covered lasagna tray and bowl of homemade salad through to the kitchen.

"Oh, the maid and the butler. There are some other staff members too, but I haven't officially met them yet. And they don't usually sleep in the servant's quarters on the premises."

"So, no one's home," I said, looking around the massive kitchen. It glistened, with white marble counter-tops and a silver overhang above the kitchen island, bearing pots and pans. The windows gave a view of the vast back yard, a path wandering through it flanked by glowing garden lights.

"No one."

"Does anyone have a key, Nelly?" Griz asked, and set down the lasagna. She peeled the foil back, and the delicious smells I'd been treated to earlier drifted up again.

"Well, yes. Grayson has a key and has had since my

mom bought the place. So have I. She said that we should be able to come see her and talk to her whenever we like. And he does, technically, own half the place, but he doesn't sleep here that often. His room's upstairs and it's empty."

I took in the information.

"Plates?" Grizzy prompted.

Nelly pointed out the relevant cupboards, and we set about preparing ourselves for the meal. The plates were laid, the lasagna reheated, the salad dished up. Finally, we were all seated around the small kitchen table off to one side. It was better than having to shout across the table in the dining hall, at least.

"Oh wow, this is delicious Grizzy," Nelly said, as she ate a bite. "You have a real talent for cooking."

"I have a question, Nelly." It had been brewing for quite some time. "Sorry." That was for Grizzy, who had been about to thank our friend for the compliment. "Where were you keeping your gun before Martha was murdered?"

Nelly had been in the process of chewing a bite of lasagna, but choked on it, now. She grabbed her glass of water and drank some. "Sorry." She coughed. "What was the question?"

I repeated it.

"Oh, I kept it here at the mansion. It was brand new. I'd never even practiced with it at the shooting range or anything. When my mom heard that Donny had bought me a gun for my protection, she suggested I keep it here."

"Why?" I asked.

"Oh, because I didn't have a gun safe at my apartment, and she had one here. It's upstairs in the master bedroom."

"Which is where?" I asked. "In relation to the crime scene, I mean."

Nelly pressed her lips together and released them slowly. "Well, it's right down the hall, actually. Two doors down."

Now, that was interesting. So the murder weapon hadn't been brought to the scene, at all. It had been here, right for the taking. And that meant that the murder had to have known where it was. Or that Martha might've had it on her person when the murderer had first entered the house.

I had no idea whether Martha's fingerprints had been on the gun or not, though. That would have at least given me some idea as to the proceedings. Just how many people had handled that gun? Nelly hadn't been arrested —did that mean her fingerprints hadn't been on the weapon? Perhaps, it had been wiped down?

Heavens, it was frustrating trying to figure this out.

"Are you all right, Chris?" Grizzy asked, as she speared a tomato slice on the end of her fork.

"Hmm? Yeah, fine. Nelly, did anyone else know the codes to the safe, apart from you and your mother?"

"I don't think so."

"But you don't know for sure?" I asked.

"Well, I don't know if my mom told the numbers to anyone else," Nelly said. "She might have, I just can't say 100%."

Which meant there was a possibility, however sparse, that Grayson had had access to the gun. Or, perhaps, one of Grayson's friends. The more I thought about it, the more suspicious he became. He'd fought with Nelly, he'd had clear motivation to murder his mother as he had clearly been down on his luck, working in the pizzeria.

The meal continued, and Grizzy engaged Nelly in idle chatter. My mind picked over the pieces, even as I shoveled a second helping of lasagna down my gullet. It was that good, and I was past being lady-like.

I needed to fuel my brain so I could work this out, once and for all.

The plates were cleared away, and we retired to the downstairs living room with coffees and a box of chocolates Nelly had bought for the evening. "They're Belgian," she said.

"I'm good, thanks," I said,. The last bit of chocolate she'd given me had literally left a bad taste in my mouth. I sipped my coffee and sat on the sofa, peering around at the grand decorations, the chandelier in the center of the room, the rich wood paneled walls and the maroon carpeting.

Nelly took a seat by the fireplace, though it was empty, now. "This is much better. Thank you so much for coming, ladies. The house is all quiet now that you're here. I'll admit, it's such a big place that it does creep me out a little. I've gone from living in a tiny one bedroom apartment over the florist's to staying in a mansion that I get lost in. Not that I'm complaining or anything, it's just … a bit big."

"I understand," Grizzy said, and sat across from her. "It must be difficult to adapt."

"How often does Grayson stay here?" I asked, and the women turned toward me, raising their eyebrows. I was so not good at small talk or at transitioning from one topic to the other.

"Oh, he comes and goes. Maybe once every two days?"

"Does he have an apartment in town?" I asked. "That he stays at when he's not here?"

"Not that I know of," Nelly replied. "But, well, I'm not exactly talking to Grayson at the moment, so I wouldn't know. I did hear through the grapevine that he left his job at the pizzeria. He's telling everyone how big he's made it because of the will." She pulled a face. "I didn't know my mother very well, but at least I didn't celebrate her death. It's horrible."

"Oh, Nelly, I wish we could help you get—"

"And where was he staying after your mother had bought the mansion?" I asked, offering Grizzy a quick and silent 'sorry' for my interruption. This was important. I might've been onto something.

"He stayed here, of course. In the house with my mother." Nelly shrugged. "She's been supporting him ever since he lost his job back in Washington."

"Interesting," I said, tapping my bottom lip.

A crash rang out from the kitchen, and we all jumped in our seats.

"What was that?" Grizzy asked.

"See what I mean? I keep hearing these noises. What if there's someone else here?" Nelly whispered.

"Then we'll confront them," I said, and rose from my seat.

$\maltese$ 15 $\maltese$

A second bang came from the hall, and I set off moving toward the doorway, forcing myself to remain calm. Likely, it was nothing but a window banging in the wind. Except, there wasn't so much as a breeze tonight.

"Chris, wait." Grizzy hurried up next to me and grasped my forearm. "Shouldn't we call the police? What if it's ... you know."

"It might be nothing," I said. "It's better to check first before we worry the police."

"I don't know." But Griz let go of my arm.

"You guys stay here."

Nelly hadn't moved from her chair—she'd gone white as a ghost and trembled on the spot, her eyes round. Her lips parted, but no words came out.

I exited into the hallway, the light from the kitchen

spilling out across the floor further along. The entrance was nearer the staircase that led up to the second floor. Nothing moved, as far as I could make out, no shadows shifting along the walls to indicate an intruder.

Grizzy appeared behind me, her jaw set. "I'm not staying behind."

"Nelly needs your help. She looks ready to throw up."

"Well, she's go about twenty maids to clean it if that does happen, so no. I'm not staying. I'm coming with you. Besides, you'll need my help even more if there is an intruder."

I appreciated the gesture, but having Grizzy with me would only worry me more. She wasn't trained to handle high pressure situations, unless they involved burgers and Mona's constant complaining. "It would be better if you stayed back, Griz."

"We're not going to argue about this. I'm coming with you."

I grunted—there was nothing else I could do—and kept on the path down the hall toward the kitchen. The closer I got, the more I tensed, but I brought my shoulders down, eased my muscles, just in case there was someone inside, waiting to pounce.

Grizzy gulped.

I turned the corner into the kitchen, checking left and right first. The lights were on, and our dishes had been placed on the counters, neatly stacked, as we'd left them. The room was empty, the tiles glistening, the countertops with their marble-white sheen. But the back door, which led out into the vast rolling grounds and down to the pool house, was open.

I frowned, coming forward.

"Careful," Grizzy whispered.

I reached the door. It was undamaged, and the short path outside was empty as well. No broken glass or mysterious stranger waiting in the darkness. "Weird," I muttered, and shut the door. I latched it this time—couldn't be sure if it had been unlocked before—and turned to Grizzy. "Looks like the coast is—"

Footsteps thumped overhead.

"I don't think that's Nelly," Grizzy whispered.

We tiptoed to the kitchen doorway.

Nelly stood outside the downstairs living room, shaking and gripping her arms to herself.

Yeah, it definitely wasn't her. The thumping continued, followed by a muffled yelp.

"What on earth?" This wasn't typical intruder behavior. The idea was to be quiet as possible to achieve one's aims. Maybe it was Grayson, who'd come home to sleep in his bedroom. That would make sense but for the yelping and bumping.

"Stay here," I said, putting out my hands to both of them. "Call the cops."

"Christie."

But I was already off up the stairs. I reached the land-ing, turned, and continued down the hall toward the source of the noise. Except it was quiet, now. I checked each room as I went, turning on the lights and finding them empty. The upstairs living room, the study, and then...

I stopped in front of the shut door to the guest room —I assumed this had to be Grayson's bedroom according to Nelly—and hesitated. I pressed my ear to the door, listening.

A click rang out, and I jerked back. There was defi-nitely someone in there. Could it be Grayson? But what would he have been yelling and thumping around for? If it was him, this would be my perfect opportunity to talk to the guy. He was my main suspect, and I hadn't yet spoken to him about the murder or his arrival in Sleepy Creek.

Come on, Christie. You know what to do.

I placed my palm to the doorknob and turned it. The door creaked open.

My jaw dropped.

Not again. No way.

The room was filled with the usual trappings of a young man's life. A desk in the corner, posters on the walls depicting bands I didn't care to identify, and a bed in one corner, the sheets rumpled and the pillow creased. The cupboards were open, clothes spilling out, and there were empty cups and an overturned ashtray beneath the open window opposite, curtains hanging white and still.

What didn't fit, however, was the dead body on the floor.

Grayson Boggs, lying face down. He'd been stabbed with what looked like an ornate letter-opener. In one hand, he grasped a golden hoop earring.

I took a breath, walked over to him, careful not to ruin any evidence, bent and pressed my fingers to his throat. No pulse.

"No!" Grizzy cried from the doorway. "Oh no, not again."

I backed away from Grayson's body and exited into the hall, trying to keep an eye on every part of the house at once, the open window—my suspicion was that the killer had escaped through it—as well as the other rooms, some of their doorways in darkness.

"This is terrible." Grizzy shook her head.

"Did you call the cops?" I asked.

I wasn't so much numb to what had happened, as I was forcing myself to remain calm. After all, if there was a killer on the loose in the house, I had to be alert. But, my guess was that they had escaped out the window.

I had to stay back, though, no matter how much I wanted to check for marks on the window sill or some means of climbing down from the second floor. If I contaminated this crime scene, Liam's lax attitude about my interferences would officially disappear.

"Griz? Did you call the cops?"

My friend was as white as Nelly had been. She nodded, at last, staring blankly at the corpse.

"Come on," I said. "Let's get downstairs and wait in the living room. There's no use standing here and staring. We should tell Nelly what happened, as well. Prepare her." But how on earth was I supposed to prepare the already terrified Nelly for this? Her long-lost brother dead.

The brother who had fought with her over their inheritance. As I guided my friend down the stairs and toward the waiting florist, I tried working it all out in my head. But my suspicions were muddled, and the case was no clearer than it had been only moments ago.

Another two murders in Sleepy Creek, and in the same family. Who was next?

$\maltese$ 16 $\maltese$

A golden hoop earring.

That was my focus as I waited tables, delivering burgers and fries, and thick malt shakes. The image of Grayson clutching that earring had stayed with me all through the night, from when Liam and Cotton had interviewed Griz, Nelly and me, to this morning when I'd woken to Curly Fries chewing on my hair.

This was a new thing she did. She got her teeth and claws tangled in my long curls and chewed and purred and massaged to her heart's content. I wasn't sure what it was about—maybe it was her way of telling me I needed a haircut—but it had only led to me washing my hair and pondering the earring, anyway.

"Hey, Watson." The call came from the corner table.

Missi and Vee sat at it, sipping on their shakes.

I trundled over. "What's up?"

"First off," Missi said, "the sky is up. Don't you ask me 'what's up' in that tone."

"Oh, do ease up, sister. I think she's got enough on her plate as it is. A full burger meal's worth of trouble."

Missi hummed under her breath and flicked her newspaper. She tried folding it, but it wouldn't bend and tuck in quite the way she desired, so she wound up squishing it into a square shape with much crinkling and muttering.

"Is she all right?"

"She doesn't like the coffee I got for the Antique Store."

"No," Missi said, lifting a finger. "You got the wrong coffee beans for the machine. There's a difference."

"I just thought we'd try something new."

"I'm eighty-years-old, Virginia. Do I look like I want to try something new?" Missi asked, pointing at the frown wrinkles on her forehead.

"You're never too old to kick a habit or pick up a new one."

"I swear, it's like living with an overly enthusiastic Labrador," Missi growled.

"For heaven's sake, Vee, get her the coffee she likes. You're threatening the happiness of everyone in Sleepy Creek by doing this," I said, the corners of my lips twitching. The twins and their idiosyncratic behavior always distracted me from my frustrations.

"Oh, you," Vee said, and grinned at me.

She'd lived with Missi's temper tantrums long enough to know that her bark was worse than her bite. Or that was my experience so far. I hadn't yet witnessed the bite and didn't plan on it for the foreseeable future.

"Sit." Missi tapped a manicured nail on the polished tabletop. "We're going to talk."

"About what?" I asked. "I've got tables to wait."

"Oh please, Watson. We both know the morning rush ended over a half hour ago."

I scanned my two remaining tables, apart from theirs, but they were occupied with reading a paper and sipping on coffee or munching on a burger.

I sat down next to Virginia, the cushy red booth chair hissing beneath me. Shoot, maybe I did need to go on a diet or start running. Apparently, worrying about the murders and mysteries in Sleepy Creek hadn't helped my waistline.

"How are you feeling?" Virginia asked.

"Like I'm missing something."

Missi pursed her lips. "A sense of accountability? A sense of service? Of..."

"Mississippi. I'm going to have to ask you to leave the table if you continue acting this way. It's one thing to poke fun, but to be downright mean is just—"

"Fine, fine," Missi sighed. "I take it back."

"Like I said, Christie, you'll have to excuse her."

"What I'm missing," I said, "is evidence. And the ability to investigate the case without jeopardizing it." And my next date with Balle. *Not that that matters or anything. It's not like I can stay in Sleepy Creek.*

"We heard about Grayson," Missi said, lowering her voice, sharp, crystal blue eyes sliding off to the left and then back again. "What a way to go. Stabbed in the back?"

"Letter opener." I fiddled with the edge of my tray, rolling it over my lap. "Window open. Second floor. Didn't get to check the garden before I left." Which would've been my first instinct. Go back and find out who had been there. Perhaps, I could find a shoe print, call in a favor with someone back in homicide to... *No, you can't do that.*

It frustrated me, having to work on these things without the proper resources. Then again, that was my fault. So, I frustrated me, in short.

"But who would have done that?" Vee asked. "And why?"

"Heard he was a horrible little man," Missi whispered, rat-tatting her nails on the tabletop next to her milkshake. "Word on the street says he spat on Maura's pizza when she came back with it to complain they hadn't put any anchovies on. He called her an 'old hag' and spat all over it. They fired him afterward."

"I had no idea," I said, tapping my chin. "Wait a second, Maura eats anchovies on her pizza?" I pulled a face.

"Yes and no, dear." Virginia chewed on the temple tip of her reading glasses. "She doesn't eat them herself, but she peels them off and puts them out for the neighborhood cats, and she feeds some to her dog, Cujo."

"Her dog is named Cujo."

"After the one in Stephen King's book," Missi said, as if I needed further explanation.

"Did she actually read the book?"

"No, dear. She didn't watch the movie either. Just thought it sounded like an interesting name," Virginia said.

Missi put up a hand. "Don't even get me started on that."

None of this had anything to do with Grayson. "Any idea who his enemies might've been?" I asked.

The hoop earring thing was stuck in my brain. I wracked it for a memory of who I'd seen wearing them. There had been Mona Jonah, for sure, and someone else. But who? Who was it?

"Not really," Missi said. "But he did have a massive fight with Janine in the pizzeria before he left. Apparently, she had just started working there, recently, and they didn't get on."

"Janine was working at the pizzeria?" Vee frowned. "That can't be right."

"They've fallen on hard times. Lost all their money. Richard's been roaming the streets looking for a job. Mona's at her wit's end having them in the house, you heard her the other day." Missi flashed a grin—any time Mona the Gossip was at wit's end was a good time for her. They were mortal enemies.

"So they fought." A piece clicked into place in my mind. Hadn't Janine been wearing hoop earrings the other day? When I'd spoken to her?

But was that a clue? How could I be sure that it had been her that had murdered Grayson based solely off an earring? I couldn't. And was Janine the type to clamber down the side of a building to escape a murder scene? From my experience, stiletto heels and short skirts weren't the best choice for speedy getaways.

Perhaps, if I spoke to Janine about what had happened? But she had been positively self-involved the last time we'd spoken. Only forthcoming with regards to her popularity and general 'awesomeness.'

"—heard the whole thing."

"What was that?"

"Oh, I was talking about the fight," Missi said. "Apparently, Bella heard the whole thing and was shocked by the animosity between the two. She's giving Janine a second chance, but well, guess it's too late for Grayson now. Bad business. These murders. The summer months are coming, and Sleepy Creek is starting to look like a very dangerous place."

Bella had overheard a conversation between Janine and Grayson. I had my next lead.

"Are you all right, Christie, dear?" Virginia asked, tapping me on the arm. "You've gone blank."

"I've got to go," I said, rising from the table. I'd ask Hedy to help me with my customers. "I've got to —just go."

"Suit yourself," Missi said, lifting her crumpled newspaper. "Mind getting us some proper coffee beans on your way back? I'll pay you for them."

"Oh for heaven's sake." Virginia took a furious sip of her vanilla milkshake.

The pizzeria was open for early lunch customers—melting cheese and crisp pepperoni was the flavor palette for my arrival. I stood in the small space in front of the counters, scanning the specials that had been attached to the walls above. They bore faded pictures of each pizza type, with prices that had been scratched out with permanent marker and written in again on the plastic front of each box.

This was how Sal's had always been, but I had to say, the pizzeria had a better vibe than it had had a few months ago when the original owner had still been alive. It was cleaner, and the young man standing behind the counter smiled at me happily.

"Welcome to Sal's Pizzeria, ma'am. May I help you?"

"Sure," I said. "Is Bella around? I'd like to speak to her."

"She's in the office, ma'am. I can fetch her for you?"

"Please."

The kid skedaddled around the counter and toward the door that had to lead through to the office. Or the staff area. He knocked once then entered. The muffled sounds of talking were barely audible over the music jiving through the speakers overhead—Elvis Presley crooning away.

A man shouted an order number in back, and a pizza was slipped onto the silver rack behind the counter—it separated front of house from back.

Finally, the kid reappeared, Bella following closely on his heels.

I kept my expression impassive, but her appearance was somewhat of a shock.

The last time I'd seen her, she'd been mourning the death of her friend, Francesca, in a black dress, her long glossy hair swaying down her back, and her eye make-up dramatic. Not to mention she'd been crying and had been threatened by a murderer—the very same Spider who had killed her friend.

Now, Bella wore her hair up in a neat bun and was fresh-faced and smiling in her Sal's Pizzeria uniform shirt —a new one with a revamped logo.

"Christie!" She gave me a hug. "It's great to see you again. To what do I owe the pleasure?"

"I was hoping to speak to you about something. In private?"

"Of course. Follow me."

We entered her office, and I took a seat on the cushy chair in front of her desk. The place was plainly decorated, with images of Sal and Fran on the walls, and a few of Bella with Fran as well. I was kind of happy for Bella.

Her involvement in the attempted murder of Dolores Baker had been called into question, but nothing had come of it yet, and no charges had been pressed against her. I'd witnessed first-hand how she'd been manipulated.

"So," Bella said, brushing her hands over her shirt, proudly. "What can I do for you?"

"Well, it's come to my attention that you witnessed a ... disagreement between Janine, your employee, and the late Grayson Boggs."

"Oh. I see." Bella flashed a sharp smile. "You're checking it out?"

"Not officially. I'm gossiping. That's all."

"Look, Christie, I'm not going to tell anyone if you want to poke around in this type of thing. If you hadn't poked around in what had happened to Franny, I might have taken the fall for it. Partly because of my own fear and stupidity."

"Right," I said.

"So, you don't have to worry about using euphemisms for 'investigation' around me. I'll tell you what you need to know."

Well, that was easy. Strangely so. Was Bella wearing hoop earrings? No, thankfully not. But she might've had a pair. Did the hoop earring narrow down the suspects to half the people in Sleepy Creek? I couldn't be so sure.

"What did you hear them arguing about, Bella? That's what I'd like to know."

Bella chewed on her bottom lip. "Let me think. They were in the front, and I heard them shouting. So I went to my door and opened it. I only caught the tail-end of their conversation, but it was somewhere along the lines of not doing something."

"Oh?"

"Yes," Bella said. "Janine was angrier than Grayson. She was like 'why are you being so dumb about this?' And Grayson told her he didn't want to be involved. He said, 'I never agreed to this, and it's not my problem anymore, so get lost.' I'm paraphrasing."

Now, that was interesting. They had been arguing over an agreement. But what could it have been? "Was there anything else?"

"Not really no. Oh wait. Yes. Janine said that Grayson owed them."

"Owed who?" I asked.

"I have no idea. Those were her direct words. 'You

owe us.' And at that point, I walked out and told them to quiet down as they had already scared off two customers. I let Grayson go. I kept Janine because it was her first offense. Grayson had been causing trouble all week. Now, I was the first one to offer him time off after what happened to Martha, but ... he wouldn't take it. He didn't seem upset about his mother's death."

That made for two children who hadn't cared about their mom passing on. Terrible. "Is there anything else you can tell me, Bella? Anything at all?"

"Nothing I can think of. Just that Grayson was the worst employee imaginable. Lazy. Never wanted to carry the extra load or help out the other staff members when they needed a break. He was selfish. Sounds mean of me to say it now that he's gone, but that's the truth."

"Thanks," I said, rising from the chair. "I appreciate you talking to me."

Bella winked. "Anything I can do to help. You were the one who helped put away Mario." She came around the desk and gave me a peck on either cheek. "If you need anything else, let me know."

"I wouldn't say 'no' to a fully-loaded pizza," I replied, chuckling, but the humor wasn't really there for me.

The talk with Bella had given me more questions than answers.

❧ 18 ❧

I tucked into one of the pizzeria's most delicious pies back at home that night, dipping the stringy cheese into my mouth, chewing thoughtfully and enjoying the saltiness of the olives and pepperoni.

Griz and Arthur had gone out on a date, and I was left with hungry beast Curly Fries, trying to work out what had happened last night. And on the night of Martha's murder. I'd made a list of my suspects, then drawn links between them according to the evidence I had, but nothing was particularly clear.

A piece was missing, as was often the case in a mystery. A link that would connect it all and drop the penny in my mind.

"Ut −ot izzit?" I asked myself, around a mouthful of pizza.

Curly Fries meowed at me and flicked her tail. She didn't like messy eating unless it was her doing it.

I tapped the end of my pen on the yellow legal pad I'd used to write up my list.

Martha had a will. She had been rich. She had left her money to Nelly and Grayson. Nelly definitely hadn't killed Grayson, not directly, at least, because she'd been downstairs with us and pale as a sheet at the moment of the murder.

And if Nelly had, say, been working with a hired killer to get rid of her brother and take all the riches for herself, why would she have called us over there? To give her an alibi. That was the obvious answer. But then, I wasn't sure she had killed him in the first place.

"More evidence," I said, after I'd swallowed my bite. "I need more evidence. And more pizza." I patted the top of another slice with a napkin, then picked it up from the grease-stained cardboard box.

So Nelly wasn't ruled out.

But what about Janine. She had had a direct confrontation with Grayson just before his murder. And she had wanted him to be a part of something and said that 'he owed them.' Whoever the 'them' was. Spiders again? No, surely not everything could be linked to my mother's case.

Then who? Her and an accomplice. Her father? But her father hadn't liked Grayson. He'd told the young man to stay away from his daughter according to Donovan. The same Donovan who had bought the initial murder weapon used in Martha's case.

I groaned around another bite of pizza. So many clues and strings, leading in different directions.

At this point, I couldn't even be certain that Grayson hadn't killed Martha either. Just because he was dead, didn't mean that he hadn't done the initial deadly deed.

Someone knocked on the front door, and I set down my pizza slice, flipped a page over the one I'd been writing on, and dabbed a napkin to my lips and fingers.

I answered the door.

"Evening." Liam stood on the doorstep, out of uniform this time, and smiling. That was a good sign. He hadn't come to accuse me of interfering again.

"Hi," I said. "What are you doing here?"

"Sheesh."

"Sorry, it's just you mentioned that we shouldn't see each other until you've solved the case. Does this mean...?"

"No," Liam said. "But I felt like seeing you in a non-professional and non-dating capacity. Call it a friendly visit. Unless you're busy?"

"Come on in." My heart did a pitter-patter, and I mentally scolded myself. He wasn't my boyfriend or anything, just someone who I got on with when he wasn't upset about my interferences. The thought of having a boyfriend was ridiculous. In Boston, I'd been too busy, and here, well, things were too complicated.

I peered out into the night before shutting the door, noting that the lights were off. Donovan wasn't home. Where was he?

Finally, I shut the front door and headed into the kitchen.

Liam had Curly Fries in his arms and was stroking her on the head.

Curly flicked her tail, but didn't meow or scratch.

"You like cats?" I asked.

"Sure," he said. "But she was about to eat the pizza slice off your plate, so I figured I'd stop that from happening."

"Shoot." Rookie mistake. I'd been living with Curly for a month, now. I should've known better than to leave the food out. "Here, give her to me."

Curly kicked up a fuss, meowing and hissing now. She bounded out of Liam's arms and streaked into the living room.

"Wow. She really doesn't like you."

"Hmm, she probably thinks I want to take my revenge," I said, which wasn't true, of course. I'd already saved Curly once, and I would never hurt an animal. She probably couldn't fathom the thought of me not wanting to get back at her for the late-night hair sucking, chewing and scalp scraping.

"Your revenge?" Liam quirked an eyebrow.

"It's a sufficiently long story," I replied.

"I've got time."

I told him, briefly, trying to eliminate as much of the humiliation from it as possible, and Liam burst out laughing by the end of it. "That's got to be the weirdest thing I've ever heard."

"Pizza?" I gestured to the half-finished pie. "Fully-loaded from Sal's."

"Don't mind if I do."

I got him a plate, poured him a glass of diet soda, and placed them both at the table. Liam thanked me and took a seat, grabbing a napkin and dabbing at the grease. "Man, I'm hungry." He took a bite and chewed, nodding to the yellow pad. "Writing poetry?"

I snorted. "I don't have a creative bone in my body, unfortunately," I said.

"I don't know about that. You're witty."

"Thanks," I said, trying not to blush. "But the only thing I create is difficult situations for me to get out of. I'm good at that." Like this one. I'd have to tell him I'd been thinking about the case, now. "I was making some, uh, notes about what happened to Martha and Grayson."

Liam sighed. "All right. Let me see 'em."

"Are you serious? No reprimand?"

"I'm off-duty. And there's only so many ways I can warn you before I just shrug my shoulders and let it be.

Besides, as long as you're not digging bullets out of walls, there's not much I can do. It's just speculation."

"I haven't dug anymore bullets out of walls," I said, trying to be reassuring but probably failing. I flipped to the page with my notes and slid it across the table.

Balle wiped his fingers off on a napkin and brought the pad closer. He studied it, his brow wrinkling. "Interesting. Any concrete deductions? This looks confused."

"That's because I'm confused. I see the links but something's missing. I have a suspect that stands out to me more than the others, though."

"And that is?" Liam took a bite of pizza, switching his gaze from the notepad to me.

"Janine Huxley. Hoop earrings. Somehow involved in this. I heard from a source that she had an argument with Grayson in the pizzeria," I said.

"Yeah, I spoke to Bella too." Liam laughed. "She was forthcoming, likely because she's scared I'll arrest her after the Mario and Dolores incident."

"Right."

"But, there's a problem with your theory," he said.

"And that is?" I leaned in.

"Janine Huxley wasn't in Sleepy Creek on the night of either murder. She was in Logan's Rest. She works a second job at a local bar in the evenings."

"Shoot." That ruined my murder prediction. But that was fine, there had to be a connection. At least, that helped rule out Janine as the murderer. But not as a conspirator. Something had been going on with Grayson and Janine.

If only I could figure out what. The frustration at not knowing would've overwhelmed me if Balle hadn't been there. So, I smiled instead, ate my pizza and chatted away. Until, eventually, the front door opened and Grizzy came in with Arthur.

The two detectives nodded to each other. Grizzy made eyes at me, and I struggled not to color.

"I'd better get going," Liam said, and rose from the table. "Thanks for the food and the company, Christie."

"Sure. Thanks for coming over. I'll see you around." I stood too but kept my distance.

Liam swept around the table and drew me into a brief hug that sent shocks and tingles to my toes. He bathed me in his lovely, woody cologne, then turned and was gone.

I had to clear my throat several times to regain my speech.

Grizzy giggled at me. Arthur grinned.

"Anyways," I said. "I'm going to bed. Night." I grabbed my notepad and headed upstairs, tapping the pen against it. The only way I'd get Liam out of my mind was if I focused on the case instead.

If only I could find out what that hoop earring was about.

19

I knocked on Nelly's front door early the next morning, carrying two cups of coffee from the Burger Bar and a divine desire for truth. That or I just hadn't gotten enough sleep last night—Curly again. I'd managed to fend her off and get her out the room, but I'd woken again at 3am to find her on my head.

She was like the Velociraptor from the first Jurassic Park. She'd figured out how to open doors, but I wasn't about to call her a 'clever girl' for it.

I stifled a yawn, stamping my feet in my sneakers on Nelly's front step. She was at her apartment this morning because the cops had cordoned off her home since, well, it was the scene of a murder. Twice over.

Finally, the latch clacked, and Nelly appeared. Her hair was a mess, falling free of a bun atop her head, and she had dark circles under her eyes. "Oh hey, Christie. Come on in. Is that coffee for me?"

My temptation was to reply with a sarcastic remark, but Nelly wasn't Missi. And she'd been through a lot. "Sure is," I said, and handed it over to her.

"Thanks for stopping by," Nelly said. "I wasn't expecting anyone, though, so you'll have to excuse the mess. You don't have a shift at the restaurant this morning?"

"Nope." I shut the door and followed her down the short hall. Nelly's apartment was full of light and potted plants. She had a cat tree in one corner, and a calico sat atop it, blinking yellow eyes at me. The living room held two armchairs and a leather sofa that had seen better days.

"I'm busy organizing a few things," Nelly said, stopping next to the coffee table. On it, a box of clothing spilled over, and next to that was a smaller golden jewelry box. Letters fell haphazardly from the edge of the table, and the armchair opposite was piled high with yet more clothes. Women's, in pastel colors.

"I'm interrupting," I said.

"No, this is nice. A surprise visit." Nelly pressed her glasses up her slightly up-turned nose. "I haven't had much company this morning. Poor Donovan has been so busy at work, and I've just been... well, I can't sleep."

"I don't blame you." Hearing a murder did that to a person.

Nelly chewed on her bottom lip. "Detective Cotton came by earlier, as well, to ask me a few questions again. I think they suspect me, Christie, and it's terrifying. I don't want anyone in Sleepy Creek to think I would ever hurt them. I just—" She removed her glasses and dabbed underneath them.

I patted her awkwardly on the arm, before taking my place on the empty armchair. "Have some coffee. That will, uh, buck you up."

"Yeah." Nelly lifted her cup and slurped on it. "I don't mean to be so morose. It's just, I lost two family members I didn't even know I had."

I nodded. "Sorry, Nelly." And I meant it—I'd lost my mom too. It wasn't easy to deal with.

"Thanks for coming." She set her coffee cup down again, on the floor next to the cat tree—very dangerous if her cat was anything like Curly Fries—and set to work folding clothing. "This is my mom's stuff. I've been meaning to organize it, but with everything going on at the mansion, I've never had the chance. I didn't want one of the staff to go ahead and do it, so..."

"I understand." The temptation to rise and poke around was almost overwhelming, but I stayed put.

"You know, it sounds silly, but I actually prefer it

here," Nelly continued. "At the mansion I always felt a bit weird."

"Because of the murders?" I asked.

"Well, yeah, that, but also it was just this vibe. Like I wasn't meant to be there or I didn't deserve to be. And it didn't help that Mr. Huxley was mailing me and telling me the same," Nelly said.

"What do you mean?" I straightened, my skin prickling.

"Nothing serious. He occasionally emailed me this week after what happened."

"About the murders?"

"No, nothing like that. Just that he tried desperately to convince me to give him the mansion back. Or sell it back to him. But I wouldn't. My mother bought it at a steal on auction. Apparently, Richard owned the mansion, but the bank foreclosed on him and auctioned off all his assets. My mother picked the place up for a steal."

This was brand-new information. Huxley was no longer well-off. What had happened to the house he'd bought? Supposedly. Janine and Grayson. Thoughts ticked, connections bridged in my mind.

Nelly lifted her mother's jewelry box, oblivious to my epiphany, and opened it. She frowned, rifling through the box, scraping metal against the insides. "That's weird."

"What?" I asked, and the skin prickling grew worse. I rose from my seat.

"There's stuff missing."

"From the jewelry box?"

"Yeah," Nelly said. "Look. The rings." She showed me the inside of the box.

And there, on the crushed velvet cushioning, sat a single golden hoop earring.

"What is it?" Nelly asked. "Good heavens, Christie, you look like you've seen a ghost."

"Nelly. Nelly, has anything else gone missing recently?" I asked. "Anything at all?"

"Well, I can't be entirely sure. I mean—"

"Do you have access to your mother's bank accounts?"

"Well, that's a rather intrusive—"

"It's important. Exceptionally important. It's got to do with the case. Did your brother have access to your mother's bank accounts?"

"No. Not that I know of. The money we were owed was put in an escrow. The executor of the will was in charge of her accounts until such a time as the murder was solved," Nelly said. "But that hasn't happened yet, obviously."

The Huxley's had fallen on hard times. Their home had been taken away. Janine had argued with Grayson about being a 'involved.' In what, a heist?

"Nelly," I said, swallowing and facing her. "Have the cops told you anything regarding your mother's murder? Anything at all?" It was so obvious, I'd never asked. I'd figured that if she wanted me to solve the murder, she would have told me outright. But that was my mistake. I was getting soft on my sabbatical. I had to step up my game. "Anything about money? Stolen items?"

"Well, yes. Apparently, the murderer took money from the safe after my mother had been... well, you know. And—"

I darted away before she could get the last part of the sentence out, the connections growing solid, now. The puzzle pieces fit.

Janine and Grayson fighting. Huxley warning Grayson away. Janine wanting Grayson involved. The safe, the gun. The Huxley's struggling to make ends meet. It all added up.

I entered Nelly's kitchen and grabbed the phone off the counter.

"What are you doing?" Nelly asked, standing in the doorway, still holding her mother's jewelry box.

"I know who did it," I said. "I'm calling Liam."

20

"Stay there, all right?" Liam had been stern but grateful about my tip-off. "I don't want you chasing after him. I'll go myself."

"And what about her?" I asked. "What if Janine causes problems?" I wasn't sure whether this had been a duo, but it seemed to me like Janine had been involved somehow. Perhaps, she hadn't murdered them outright, but she had known. She had to have known that her father had been desperate enough to commit those murders.

"Stay with Nelly. If you're right about this, she could very well be a target. I'm sending Arthur over, just in case."

"Thank you."

He hung up, and I put the phone down.

Nelly was white around the lips and clutching her

mother's jewelry box to her chest. "You really think it was them?" she asked.

"Liam said he'd been keeping tabs on both Janine and Richard, and that he'd just received news that they'd gone missing an hour ago when I called. They were already on their way out to find them."

"Oh my gosh. I can't believe it. But what about Grayson? How was he involved?" Nelly asked.

I didn't want to upset her more than she already was.

"Christie?"

"Grayson may have worked with Richard. I can't be sure. We'll see what Liam says. He's the one with the hard evidence." Heavens knew if I'd had any of it, it would have made reaching this conclusion much easier. My best guess was that the cops didn't have enough to bring Huxley down, but they had their suspicions.

And after Grayson's murder, well, it wouldn't have taken much to spook Huxley into leaving. Perhaps, it had been a mistake.

Grayson had 'owed' them. Had he been in the process of stealing from Nelly when it happened? If only I had gone through and checked the safe in the upstairs living room after the murder. But no, I'd been too preoccupied with my own thoughts.

Getting soft. I would have to toughen up if I ever planned on solving my mother's case. Thankfully, from what I could tell, neither Huxley nor Nelly's brother were from Boston. They weren't Spiders, and that meant this case was an unfortunate coincidence, given that there had been such a long string of murders prior to it.

"I need to lie down. Or sit down. I just—" Nelly swayed on the spot.

"Here," I said. "Let me help you. You lie down. You want something to drink? Aspirin? A glass of milk?" That was what you gave to a person to calm them down, right?

"No, I just need to lie down. And... are you going to leave?"

"No, Nelly. I'm staying. I'll hang out in the living room, if that's OK."

"Yeah, that's great." Nelly's shoulders sagged out of relief. "Sorry, Christie."

"No way. It's perfectly fine." I walked her through to her bedroom, checked the curtains and windows were closed, then exited and left her in the dark. I took a seat on the worn leather sofa, staring at the clothing spilling from the boxes.

So, it had been Richard all along. Perhaps Janine too. And Grayson?

The evidence stacked in my mind, but I didn't have much to go on here. And now, I had to sit, quite frustratingly, on Nelly's sofa and wait for Liam to swoop in and take care of it. But what if Huxley got away?

Shoot, how could I have not seen it before?

Nelly had mentioned that her attacker on the night

of Martha's murder had been tall and wiry. Huxley was exactly that, and hadn't we seen him hanging around outside Candy's gun store on the afternoon we went to ask about the purchases?

Grayson had to have known the code for the safe. Perhaps, Martha had walked in on him stealing from her and taken exception to that? He had then turned the gun on her and...

It was all speculation.

I missed having the necessary information to close a case now more than ever. But this was it. I'd wait for Arthur to get here. There was nothing more I could do.

I flopped back in the armchair.

The cat on the cat-tree rose from its sitting position. Its hair stood on end and it gave a low growling meow.

"Huh?" I turned, but it wasn't focused on me.

It leaped off the stand and streaked out of sight, into Nelly's bedroom.

"What was that about?" Had she smelled Curly Fries on me? Or maybe, I was just the anti-cat.

A creaking noise sounded from down the hall. That definitely hadn't come from Nelly's room. I frowned, rising from my armchair, and those prickles were back. Liam had mentioned looking out for Nelly. That Arthur would come over soon.

What if Richard Huxley hadn't left Sleepy Creek at all?

I took a slow step around the coffee table, keeping my breathing even and my ears pricked for any sounds.

A snore came from Nelly's room, and I stopped in the doorway, peering in. The woman had fallen asleep on the bed—the stress of it all had probably knocked her out. Her arm was thrown over her face. Her cat sat on top of the dresser, peering down at me with those glowing yellow eyes.

I shook my head and walked back into the living room. It was my paranoia, or my desperate hope that I could somehow be a part of the final capture of Huxley. That was all.

I lifted my Styrofoam coffee cup from the table and turned it in circles against my palms. It was almost cool, but I took a sip anyway, grimacing.

Another creaking noise then a scrape.

"What is that?" I whispered.

Silence again.

"Am I losing my mind?" *You're talking to yourself. That's pretty much a given at this point.*

Nelly's snoring started up again, and I forced myself to relax. Huxley was on his way out, and I was stuck here. That was the honest truth of it and that was—

The *crash* came from behind me. I dropped my coffee mug and spun toward the sound.

A door stood open opposite the living room, and Janine was in it, wearing two hoop earrings and a mask of fury. The wrought-iron fire escape clanged beneath her steps. She held a fire poker, squeezing and twisting so that her knuckles turned white.

"You interfering cow," she said, and stepped into the room. "It's about time I got rid of you."

❦ 21 ❦

In the past two seconds, I had come to a not-so-astounding conclusion: it was safe to say that Janine had been involved in either Martha or Grayson's murder.

I'd asked for hard evidence, and, boy, did I have it now.

Janine tossed her bottle blonde hair and pranced into the room, holding that fire poker like it was a baton or a prop in some elaborate dance she was about to put on for me.

And I had nothing but the cat-tree for protection. Dance or no dance, Janine's eyes said one thing and one thing only: "I'm going to murder your interfering booty."

"Janine," I said. "Good to see you again."

"You weirdo," she replied.

"That represents a certain degree of irony, wouldn't

you say? You're holding a fire poker and wearing stilettos."

"Always look good for work," Janine replied, grinning at me.

"Murder is a job for you? When did you add it to your resume?"

"Don't, like, try to get smart with me. I didn't murder anybody, OK? Like, that is not my M.O. I just do what I have to do to get what I want."

"And what do you want?" I asked, backing away slowly, stepping around the coffee table and putting it between us.

Janine tottered forward, still squeezing that fire poker. Its sharp end was rusted, and I didn't doubt a swift jab to the arm would lead to a tetanus shot, assuming I didn't die from it. I had to keep her preoccupied. Arthur would be here soon.

And the more I got out of her the better. I'd have something to tell him when he arrived, and he'd have caught her red-handed. This was attempted murder, at least.

"What I want is what I deserve. Like, I was raised with a certain standard of living, and I'm going to get that."

"Did you murder them?" I asked. "Or was it your dad, alone?"

Janine laughed. A cackle that would've suited a witch.

"Did I murder them? I never get my hands dirty. I get my hands full of ice, ice baby." She freed one hand from the poker and wiggled the various jeweled rings on it. "I don't have to tell you anything."

"But you fooled us all." It was the flattery tactic. Hopefully, Janine was stupid enough to fall for it. "I was so sure it was your dad who murdered everyone. That he was the mastermind behind it all."

"Dad killed Grayson," she said, flippantly.

"And Grayson killed Martha," I replied. "For money. For you."

"For both dad and me." Janine shrugged. "Grayson realized that we were who he needed. See, Grayson was, like, my boyfriend, but he was so super stupid. He never even clicked that, like, a woman like me does not date a lowlife like him. We used him and then we dumped him. Simple."

I nodded. "That's smart." *Get more out of her. Keep her talking. Arthur will be here soon.*

He surely wouldn't arrive with his sirens ringing, but gosh, was he taking his time.

"You're right it's smart. We used him, and now, my dad's gone. You'll never see him again. So there."

"Did you get what you wanted, Janine? Did you get the money?"

Her lips thinned into a white line because, of course, she hadn't. Her father had murdered Grayson before the murder could be solved, and that meant they hadn't gotten any money from the lawyers. Their only option had to be to get it from Nelly. And that was why Janine was here.

Had to be.

The cops would arrest Richard. Janine would use Nelly to phone the lawyer and get that money released, now that an arrest had been made. That was what she thought. And that made her a pea-brain.

"You're not supposed to be here," Janine said. "You're in the way." She lifted the poker, bracing it in her grasp. Prepping to swing. "Now, I have to get rid of you."

"C'mon, we both know you're not the one who does the dirty work," I said. "You're the brains behind the operation."

She came forward. "I, like, know what you're doing." She swung the fire poker at me.

I ducked, and it whistled over my head. My palms grew slick with sweat. I dropped to the floor and rolled behind the sofa, rose again, and scrambled toward the hall, but Janine blocked my path. Her eyes were wide now, her pupils dilating. She lifted the poker again.

I had nowhere to go but back. My heels bumped the sofa's side.

Janine grinned.

Trapped,

A figure appeared in the doorway to the bedroom.

Nelly, her glasses askew, her teeth bared. She yelled wordlessly and dived toward Janine. Her arms connected with the stiletto-queen's midriff, and the pair crashed to the floor.

I tripped backward over the sofa to avoid the collision and one of my sneakers flung off the end of my foot. It turned end over end once and smacked me on the nose. Bad, but better than having my face broken in with a fire poker.

"Get off! Get off me, you witch," Janine shrieked.

"Christie, I've got her." Nelly's yell was strangled.

I sprang upward.

Nelly had one hand pressing Janine's face into the carpet and sat astride her back. Janine kicked and gasped, turning her head this way and that. Her hand reached for the fire poker, which had rolled under the coffee table during the altercation.

I kicked it further away. "Rope?"

"Cable ties in the kitchen drawer," Nelly said, heaving breaths as Janine bucked and screeched.

I was into the kitchen and back again as fast as I could manage. "Get her arms behind her back." I slipped the cable-tie over her wrists and tightened it in place. "OK, Nels, you can get off now."

Nelly slid sideways. She exhaled and grew pale all over again, staring wide-eyed at Janine. Perhaps, the enormity of what had just happened had hit home.

"Thanks for saving my neck," I said, rubbing the sore spot on my nose where the sneaker had hit. I slipped the offending shoe back onto my foot.

"You can't do this to me," Janine screamed. "You can't—"

A banging started up at the front door. "Sleepy Creek police. Open up!"

"There's Arthur." I settled the sneaker back on my foot. "I'll get it. You, uh, make sure she doesn't try anything."

And that was it. Another two cases solved, the murderers soon to be behind bars, assuming Liam had gotten his hands on Mr. Huxley.

I was left with one question and one question alone: would there ever be a peaceful, murder-free week in Sleepy Creek?

** 22 **

The Burger Bar buzzed with activity. The end of a long week had come, and Grizzy had the restaurant open for brunches and lunches after church. Folks sat in their Sunday best, slurping down milkshakes, sipping on coffees, eating their Breakfast Burgers and their fries.

I leaned against the counter, keeping an eye on my tables, my tray tucked under one arm, and the load significantly lighter on my shoulders than it had been all week.

The case was closed.

The Huxley's had been imprisoned, though Janine would likely get a lighter sentence than her father since she hadn't done any of the murdering herself. And because she'd squeal on her dad. I wouldn't put anything past her.

"Well, well, well, what do we have here?" Missi had

arrived, and she bore a frown that wrinkled her already creased brow to the maximum degree. "Just what I expected. A Watson. A Watson who knows exactly how to ruin my afternoon."

"What have I done now?" I asked.

"Oh, I think you know exactly what you've done," Missi said.

Virginia stepped up beside her sister, patting her curls into place. "Don't worry about her, dear, she's just mad that Mona is back at church and smiling."

"What did you do?" Missi asked. "The woman was finally out of my hair. Finally out of the way. And now…"

"Excuse me for help bringing two murderers to justice." I explained about the Huxleys, in brief, and Vee gasped.

"I can't believe we hadn't heard about this. There must have been a breakdown in the gossip vine," she said.

"Likely because Mona wasn't around to head it this week. See, Missi? It's a good thing I helped solve the case, after all." I wiggled my eyebrows at her.

"Debatable at best. I've got my eye on you, Watson." She marched off to her usual table, shooing customers and poor Hedy, our newest waiter, out of the way. She plonked her butt down in the booth that was reserved for the terrible twins on Sundays and picked up the newspaper from the tabletop.

"Don't mind her, dear. She's just angry that the respite

from Mona's ministrations is over. Oh well. Two shakes please? Of the usual flavor. And a Breakfast Burger each will go down heavenly. You'll see, after she's gotten some food in her system she'll be back to her normal self."

"So, just as grumpy then?"

"Don't you start." Virginia pinched my cheek then patted it. "Good job on the case, dear. And on not getting caught interfering."

"I can't get caught if I practically hand myself over," I said.

Virginia hurried off to join her sister, and I put in their order with Grizzy behind the milkshake bar and Jarvis in the kitchen. The sizzle of patties, the hum and hubbub of chatter, and the clink of forks was the perfect ending to a seriously weird week.

I kept myself busy serving up burgers to my tables, sometimes trying for a smile, other times barely hearing what they said. The fact was, the case was solved, but I still hadn't gotten any closer to solving my mother's murder.

It had truly gotten under my skin now. The choice was clear: find a way to investigate it and lose my job, or do nothing and potentially watch as more people in town got hurt.

The Huxley's might not have been connected to my mother's case, but the mystery the week before definitely had been.

The afternoon arrived, and the yellow light that came with it brightened the interior of the Burger Bar, warming it and me too. Things had to get better. They would, and I'd had a pretty great birthday week all things considered. A new book, time with my best friend, and—

"Christie." Liam's cologne hit me smack-dab in the nose, and I inhaled deeply.

Boy, when had I started sniffing the guy? This had gone too far.

My insides did the twist and flip. I turned from the milkshake bar and smiled at him. "Hi," I said. "Come in for an afternoon snack? Or is this one of those 'I'm reporting you to your superiors' chats?"

"Neither," he replied, and took a seat on one of the barstools, looking as handsome as ever in a fitted white t-shirt and a pair of blue jeans. The man had muscles. And I had to keep my eyes on his face or I'd wind up humiliating myself.

"Oh? Then what can I help you with?"

"I wanted to give you a birthday gift," he said. "But I didn't know what was appropriate, given that we're not... anything. Friends, I guess, is the best way to put it."

There went my stomach again.

"So, tough to get you a gift."

"You really don't have to," I said. "I'm fine with no gifts. I've never been good with accepting them anyway. So. That's fine. Do you want a milkshake? Burger?"

"Well, shoot. I did get you a gift. Now, I'm wondering if I should have at all."

I licked my lips. "What is it?" If it was jewelry, I wouldn't handle it well. That seemed so serious, and we'd only just started dating.

"I spoke to my captain. I'm reopening your mother's cold case, and I'm the lead detective," he said. "I'll need to consult with you on it, frequently, since you were the only one around at the time who might have seen anything. I might even be able to show you pictures, documents. Won't need to talk to your superiors in Boston either."

Heat flushed through my body from the tips of my toes, all the way up to my head. "Are you...? Are you serious, Liam?" My throat tightened. "You did that?"

"Yeah," he said. "Is it a good gift?"

I leaped off my stool and threw my arms around his neck, my tray clattering to the floor. "Thank you," I said. "Thank you so much." Tears came—I never cried—and I couldn't stop them. "You have no idea how much this means to me."

He drew me to his chest and hugged me tight. "I want to help you," he said, into my hair. "In any way I can."

"Hey! Get a room, you two," Missi called.

"What's going on?" Grizzy asked, as she rounded the milkshake bar again after having been in the office.

I told her as Liam slung his arm around my shoulders and held me to his side. Grizzy clapped her hands, Missi and Vee came over to find out what was going on, and I closed my eyes, taking in the moment.

Finally, I'd have the chance to find out the truth. And it was all thanks to Liam, to Sleepy Creek, and to the people I cared about the most.

But I'd get to the investigating later. "Let's have a round of milkshakes," I said. "With extra cherries on top."

"Coming right up," Grizzy said, and grinned.

We served the last of the customers then closed the Burger Bar early and sat down at one of the longer tables together, me next to Liam, Missi and Vee with Griz. Jarvis came out to toast to another good week of sales, burgers, and a case solved.

I'd come back, alone, to take a break from work, dreading Sleepy Creek and my mother's cold case. Chaos had ensued. And somehow, in the middle of it all, I'd found myself a family.

"To next week," Grizzy said, raising her milkshake glass.

"To next week," we echoed.

Who knew what it would bring?

Christie's adventures continue in *the Salmon Burger Murder*.

CRAVING MORE COZY
MYSTERY?

If you had fun with Charlie and Gamma, you'll want to meet Milly and her pet bunny Waffle. You can read the first chapter of Milly's story below!

"It's unheard of! A travesty." My grandmother, Cecelia Pepper, sat on the edge of her seat at the coffee bar in the Starlight Cafe. "Why, the sheriff ought to be ashamed of himself. How are we meant to walk down the streets in this town with this... threat in the backs of our minds? Looming! Like some giant Sword of Damocles over our heads." She tapped the newspaper, a copy of *The Star Lake Gazette*, she'd laid on the coffee bar the minute she'd sat down.

My grandmother was the definition of dynamite in a small package. At 75-years-old, she was brimming with vigor to make up for her height.

"I'm sure Sheriff Rogers will figure it out." I fixed Gran a cup of coffee—a hazelnut latte with extra cream —and placed it in front of her. "It's a small town, Gran. They'll catch whoever's doing this."

"A small town that's going downhill quickly." My grandmother glanced around as if she was afraid of someone overhearing our conversation.

But the painful truth was there was nobody in my cafe this morning. Just like there'd been nobody in it the day before.

As I'd learned quickly, folks in Star Lake, Iowa, were insular. They didn't care that my late father, a town favorite, had left me the cafe. I hadn't lived in town long enough for them to trust me, and then there was the fact that I had absolutely no experience in the hospitality industry.

Not now. Just take a breath and smile.

"I mean, really. A mugger? Here? Nancy from the bakery told me her sister's best friend's cousin was attacked. Wallet stolen. Can you believe that? If I didn't love the lake and the people so much," my grandmother continued, lifting the latte, "I'd move away in a heartbeat."

"Gran."

"I'm serious."

"Gran, you've lived here for thirty-five years."

"Fine. I might not move, but I'll protest this at the

next town council meeting. You can mark my words on that." Gran took a sip of her latte, pressed her lips together and fluttered her eyelashes. "Nearly as good as your father used to make."

A silence ensued, filled with our shared sorrow. It was too soon to talk about him.

I cast my gaze away from Gran and studied the interior of the cafe. Light streamed through the windows and the glass front doors, illuminating the linoleum that was in need of a revamp, as well as the checked tablecloths and laminated menus. The chairs were comfortable and well worn. The cash register was an antique and the walls were dark wood.

Overall, the aesthetic was typical of my dad's taste. Hastily thrown together but with plenty of heart.

"This really is good." Gran must've noticed the lump in my throat. Metaphorically, of course. "You know, you'll make a fine restaurant owner. As fine an owner as you would've made a detective."

That was another touchy subject. "Thanks, Gran." I forced a smile.

She reached over and patted my forearm.

Movement outside on the brick-paved sidewalk caught my attention. A homeless woman, wearing a shabby coat and carrying several plastic bags, walked up and took a seat outside the cafe.

"Oh dear," Gran said.

"Do you know her?"

"Only by sight," Gran replied. "She's new to town I think. I'm not familiar with her story. Poor woman."

I bit down on my lip then headed back to the coffee machine and started fixing another latte. Much to my surprise, the bell over the door tinkled, and Sheriff Rogers entered.

He was in his late fifties, with a gray mustache, balding, and wearing his uniform with pride. He sauntered over to the bar and eyed me. "Morning."

"Good morning, Sheriff," I said. "What can I get for you today?"

The sheriff didn't immediately answer me. He scanned the interior of the cafe then pointed over to a new section I'd set up, with the help of my cook, Francesca. "What's that?"

"That's the waffle station," I said, smiling. "Do you want to try it out? We prepare the waffles fresh, bring 'em out to you, and then you decorate them as you see fit. There's ice cream and maple syrup, there's—"

"That wasn't here when Frank was running the place."

"No," I said. "No, it wasn't. I figured that people would enjoy—"

"Waffles?"

"Sheriff Rogers," my grandmother said, and the sheriff jumped a little.

"Celia." He sniffed, using Gran's nickname. "Shoot. I

didn't see you there." And he sounded truly regretful, like he was anticipating a volley of complaints. He wouldn't have been wrong in that respect.

"What's this I hear about a mugger?" Gran tapped the newspaper. "A mugger in our midst?"

"Well, yeah, there have been reports of muggings over the past week, but I assure you it's under control."

"Now, Sheriff, you know better than to shovel that level of manure around me," Gran said. "I want answers, and I want them now. What am I supposed to tell the ladies in my book club? That we can't walk to the library in peace?"

"I assure you..."

The conversation faded out as I finished off the latte, grabbed a cupcake from the display of about a dozen under the glass counter, and walked out into the sunlight.

It was the end of summer, the weather a temperate 70 degrees with a soft breeze brushing down the street. I stopped in front of the homeless woman.

"Good morning," I said.

She glared at me, her skin tan, and her ire obvious. "What do you want, Red?"

The urge to brush my fingers through my red hair nearly overtook me. Thankfully, my hands were full. "Uh."

"Let me guess. You want me to move. It's a free country, you know, I—"

"No," I said. "I just wanted to check if you were OK."

"OK?"

"Yeah." I handed her the coffee and the cupcake. "You need anything?" It was my experience, after working as a beat cop in the city, that everyone had a story. Just like everyone had a purpose. Sometimes life just... got in the way.

The woman blinked. "Uh. Yeah. I'm good. Thanks."

"Sure. Just holler if you need a glass of water or something," I said. "I'll be inside."

The woman, still full of mistrust, nodded then took a sip of her coffee. I headed back into the cafe and found Gran and Sheriff Rogers embroiled in their argument.

"—muggers on the streets. If you think that we'll stand for this then you're delusional. You know, I can call up the heads of the three factions, right now, and get them to arrange a meeting."

Sheriff Rogers, blustery as he was, paled at that.

The "factions" as they were called, were the three unions that pretty much ran Star Lake. There were "the boaters", "the butchers", and "the bakers"—and they frequently disagreed on issues, to the point where the town was practically split into three. It was expected that you'd fall into line with one of the groups even if you weren't an active member of said union.

"The bakers would be most interested to hear about your lack of action when it comes to crime on our streets. I mean, this whole area is packed with bakeries and restaurants. This is bound to affect tourism too. And then the boaters will get antsy."

The summer months in Star Lake were famed for their fun boating activities, from tours on the lake, to fishing, to jet skiing and recreational activities.

"You're complaining about mugging and crime on the street," Sheriff Rogers said, finding his voice, "yet you won't stop your granddaughter over here from feeding said criminals."

Gran jerked back as if she'd been slapped—a strange effect on a tiny woman in a floral-print dress. "Feeding them? I think the heat is getting to you, Sheriff."

"She just took out a coffee and a cupcake to..." He trailed off and gestured toward the homeless woman now sitting on a bench out front.

"And so?" Gran grew red and rose from her barstool, trying to tower at four feet eight inches.

The sheriff tugged on his collar. "All I'm saying is that if you don't want trouble, don't invite it into your home." And with that, he swept from the cafe, trailing his overbearing spicy cologne.

"Idiot," Gran muttered.

"Gran."

"There's no love lost between us." She resumed her seat. "And for good reason."

But she didn't go into the reason. I fixed a cup of

coffee for Francesca, who was in the kitchen, patiently awaiting orders that would likely never come, and then joined my grandmother at the counter.

Gran paged through the newspaper, stopping on an image and tapping it. "See, now, this is why you don't want to get on the wrong side of those boaters. Look at that. A full page ad for their 'Boating Blowout 2021.'"

I read over her shoulder. "Join us for a boating extravaganza as we celebrate the end of summer."

"You're going, I assume? Everyone's going," Gran said. "Everybody who's anybody. It will be a great opportunity for you to network, dear. It's been a year, and you've only made one friend."

"Thanks, Gran."

"I'm just saying," she replied, "that it might be a good opportunity for you to get out there and meet someone."

"Meet someone? The only person I'm interested in meeting is an accountant who can help me manage my finances for this place." Things were *not* looking good. And I was *not* about to let down my father's legacy by losing the Starlight Cafe.

"I'm sure there are plenty of eligible accountants around."

"Not what I meant, Gran."

She gave me a sneaky smile, and it cheered me up. I couldn't stay mad at Gran.

"Are you coming by tonight for supper?" Gran asked.

"I'm making chicken casserole. You can bring Waffle along."

"That sounds great."

It sure beat eating a microwave dinner over the kitchen sink.

Want to read more? You can grab **the first book on all major retailers.**

Happy reading, friend!

PAPERBACKS AVAILABLE BY ROSIE A. POINT

A Burger Bar Mystery series

The Fiesta Burger Murder

The Double Cheese Burger Murder

The Chicken Burger Murder

The Breakfast Burger Murder

The Salmon Burger Murder

The Cheesy Steak Burger Murder

A Bite-sized Bakery Cozy Mystery series

Murder by Chocolate

Marzipan and Murder

Creepy Cake Murder

Murder and Meringue Cake

Murder Under the Mistletoe

Murder Glazed Donuts

Choc Chip Murder

Macarons and Murder

Candy Cake Murder

Murder by Rainbow Cake

<u>*A Milly Pepper Mystery series*</u>

Maple Drizzle Murder

<u>*A Sunny Side Up Cozy Mystery series*</u>

Murder Over Easy

Muffin But Murder

Chicken Murder Soup

Murderoni and Cheese

Lemon Murder Pie

<u>*A Gossip Cozy Mystery series*</u>

The Case of the Waffling Warrants

<u>*A Mission Inn-possible Cozy Mystery series*</u>

Vanilla Vendetta

Strawberry Sin

Cocoa Conviction

Mint Murder

Raspberry Revenge

Chocolate Chills

<u>*A Very Murder Christmas series*</u>

Dachshund Through the Snow

Owl Be Home for Christmas

www.ingramcontent.com/pod-product-compliance
Lightning Source LLC
Chambersburg PA
CBHW030959210726
48290CB00007B/2379